"I came out here
Stacy's mother said.

"About what?" Lane asked.

"Well, you and Stacy are . . . seeing each other?"

"Does that bother you?"

"Not because I have any serious objection to you, but she's used to a different life-style, and I wanted to make sure that she wasn't staying here just to keep from hurting you."

"Stacy wants to leave?"

"I haven't yet had a chance to talk to her. I thought I'd try to understand what was going on here before I tried to advise her."

Lane took a deep, uneven breath. "Mrs. Blair," he said firmly, "Stacy's free to leave whenever she wants to go. I won't stand in her way."

"Stacy's mother smiled. "Thank you, Lane. That's all I wanted to know."

Books by Brenda Cole

Alabama Moon
Larger Than Life
Don't Fence Me In
Tomorrow and Tomorrow
Hunter's Moon
Spoiled Rotten
Three's A Crowd
Foreign Exchange
Alabama Nights

BRENDA COLE was born and grew up in rural Alabama, the setting for many of her novels. The third of four daughters, she lived for many years on a small farm. She graduated from Greensboro High School and went on to Livingston University for a degree in English Education. Subsequently, she taught English in junior and senior high schools. After her marriage she traveled all over the country with her husband. They now live in San Jose, California.

BRENDA COLE

Alabama Nights

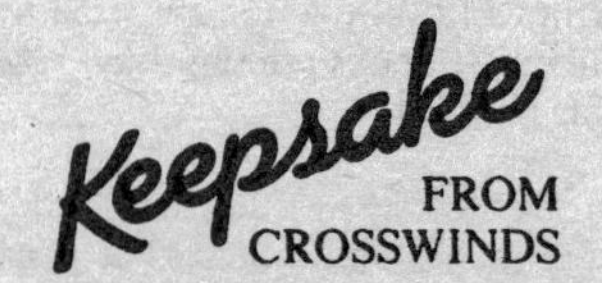

New York • Toronto • Sydney
Auckland • Manila

First publication December 1988

ISBN 0-373-88037-5

Printed in the U.S.A.

RL 4.5, IL age 11 and up

Dear Reader:

Welcome to our line of teen romances, Keepsake from *CROSSWINDS*. Here, as you can see, the focus is on the relationship between girls and boys, while the setting, story and the characters themselves contribute the variety and excitement you demand.

As always, your comments and suggestions are welcome.

The Editors
CROSSWINDS

Chapter One

Glancing down to turn on her left blinker, Stacy noticed that she had chipped a fingernail. "Oh, great," she muttered to herself, "Mother's never going to believe that just happened."

Instinctively she curled her fingers around the steering wheel—not that it would do any good to try to hide it. Where grooming was concerned, nothing got past Diane Blair.

Stacy knew her only hope was to reach the airport in time to repair the damage before her mother's plane landed. After all, she wanted everything about this weekend to be as perfect as possible. She didn't want to give her mother any reason to regret letting her live with her aunt and uncle and finish high school in Alabama.

Not that she had always felt that way. At the beginning of last summer, when her parents announced that they were getting a divorce and sending her to spend the summer with her Aunt Sara and Uncle Jim on their farm in Alabama, Stacy was inconsolable. She had pleaded with her parents to let her stay with Joni Bothel, her best friend from boarding school, but they were adamant about keeping her away from the unpleasantness of the divorce.

By the end of summer, Stacy had to admit that her parents had been right all along. It took time for her to reconcile herself to their divorce, but getting acclimated to life on a farm, and three younger cousins, made it impossible for her to dwell on her unhappiness. And then, there was Lane.

Just as her mother and Aunt Sara were sisters, Lane's father and Uncle Jim had been brothers. However, both of Lane's parents had been killed in an automobile accident when he was much younger. Now he lived with his grandmother, Uncle Jim's mother, and helped his uncle run the family farm.

When they first met, Stacy had thought Lane was rude and obnoxious, and Lane had made it clear that he considered her totally useless. They spent most of the summer avoiding each other, and just when they discovered their mutual attraction, it was time for Stacy to return home to Philadelphia.

Only, there was no home. After the divorce, Stacy's father had rented a small apartment near his office, and her mother had taken a job and moved to Washington, D.C. They had planned for Stacy to return to the boarding school she had been attending and to alternate her vacations between them. At the last minute, Stacy had convinced them to let her stay in Summerdale and graduate from her mother's alma mater in nearby Douglasville.

Just as Stacy turned into the airport's parking lot, she saw a large commercial plane landing. Sheffield was considerably larger than any of the surrounding small towns, but even it didn't have a lot of air traffic. She knew that plane must be the one bringing her mother and her best friend to spend the Thanksgiving holidays with her at the Colbys'.

Stacy pulled into the first available parking space and hurried into the terminal just in time to catch her mother and Joni as they came through the swinging doors.

"Stacy!" her mother called, rushing toward her.

As usual, Diane Blair looked as if she had just stepped off the cover of a fashion magazine. Her golden brown hair, lightly peppered with gray, was carefully styled into a short, sculptured coiffure, and the silk scarf draped over her shoulder added just the right touch to her well-tailored suit.

Joni, in a navy blazer and camel skirt, was just as fashionable. Her dark hair fell below her shoulders in a smooth, straight line, accentuating the carefully made-up face with its dark, sooty lashes and vibrant red lipstick.

Suddenly Stacy felt self-conscious about her own appearance. She was wearing a simple corduroy skirt and sweater. Her short, naturally curly, brown hair refused to remain smooth for very long, and what makeup she had carefully applied that morning had long since worn off.

It was her last conscious thought before she threw herself into their arms. Then they were all talking at once.

"I've missed you!"

"I can't believe you're really here!"

"You look wonderful!"

Diane fussed over Stacy, fluffing her hair, smoothing her collar and brushing imaginary lint from her shoulders. "You've grown so much," she said.

"Oh, Mother," Stacy protested. "I haven't grown an inch. Besides, I was home just three months ago."

"I know, but now you're all the way across the country. That makes it different."

Stacy smiled and rolled her eyes at her friend. "Joni, how many times have you been home since school started?"

"Once. I went home in October to get some things for my dorm room, and a Halloween costume for a party we were having at school."

"See, I've actually saved you money by living with Aunt Sara," Stacy said. She led the way to the baggage claim to collect her mother's three bags and Joni's two.

"I thought you were only staying for four days," Stacy said.

"We are," her mother replied. "One of these bags is full of things for you. Of course, if you want me to leave it here..."

"That's all right," Stacy said quickly. "I brought the station wagon, so there's plenty of room for all of them."

In the parking lot, Diane looked at the car apprehensively. "It's so big," she said.

"Don't forget, Aunt Sara and Uncle Jim have three children of their own, and now that I'm living with them, there are six of us in all. Hal's fourteen now, and Chris is eleven, and they take up as much room as two adults. Plus, Angie's already six, so she's no baby.

It takes a large car for all of us to go anywhere together."

"I just can't believe they let you drive it all the way from Summerdale by yourself."

"Uncle Jim lets me drive the tractor, too, and it's twice as expensive as this car," Stacy said.

They got into the car, but before Stacy started the engine, her mother handed her a small fingernail file.

"Why don't you smooth out that fingernail before you do anything else?"

"Mother, no one's going to see it between here and home," Stacy protested.

"Maybe not, but it won't take you but a moment to take care of it. If you don't do something about it now, you might forget it."

Stacy gave in and repaired the nail.

As soon as they were out of Sheffield, and she could afford to relax, Stacy pulled Joni into the conversation. "How are things at school this year? Any changes at dear old Brantwood?"

"No, everything's pretty much the same. Of course, there are certain privileges of being a senior. I'm rooming with Shari Benson now, and we've been allowed to go to some of her brother's football games at Penn State."

All Stacy could remember about Shari Benson was that she had bleached blond hair and low grades, but if Joni was happy with her, she certainly wasn't going to say anything against her.

"What about you?" her mother asked. "You didn't cut school to drive over here to meet us, did you?"

"I'm going to Douglasville High, remember?" Stacy asked with a short laugh. "It's impossible to skip school when everyone in town knows your name, grade and probably your schedule. Three people stopped me before I got out of town to ask if everything was all right at home."

"The infamous grapevine," her mother murmured. "That was one of the reasons I couldn't wait to get away. I wanted to go somewhere where I could be just an anonymous face in the crowd."

"I don't mind it," Stacy said. "Sometimes they're nosy, but they care. And in answer to your question—no, I didn't cut school. Aunt Sara called and got me excused from my afternoon classes. I saw Miss Anderson before I left school and got my English assignment."

"Miss Anderson? Evelyn Anderson?" her mother asked. "I didn't know she was still teaching. I had her when I was in the twelfth grade."

"I know. She told me," Stacy said, "and she sends her love to you."

Joni moved up to rest her arms on the back of the front seat. "Excuse me, but I'm confused. I address my letters to you in Summerdale, but when Mrs. Blair made our plane reservations, she said we were flying to Sheffield. Now, you two are talking about Douglasville. Exactly where are we now?"

"It's not really that complicated," Stacy said with a laugh. "We just left Sheffield. It's the only city around here, and fortunately it has an airport that can handle anything besides crop dusters or private planes. We usually come here when we want to do any serious shopping or have dinner at a really nice restaurant. Douglasville is the closest . . . town to the farm. That's where I go to school, and we do our grocery shopping and that kind of thing. Summerdale is the name of the community where Aunt Sara and Uncle

Jim live. It has a post office and a combination general store and gas station. See, it's simple."

"Then why are we driving away from civilization? I don't even see any houses."

"I felt the same way the first time I came here," Stacy said. "But don't worry, you'll see some houses pretty soon."

As they rounded the next curve, Stacy saw a pickup truck stopped just off the pavement. The driver was sitting on the hood, and as they passed him, he raised his hand and waved.

Stacy immediately slowed down and signaled her intention to pull off the road.

"Stacy, what are you doing?" her mother asked. "You know better than to stop along a public highway and pick up a stranger."

Stacy was already rolling down her window. "It's all right, Mother, I know him from school."

The boy was ambling toward the car, and Stacy raised her voice to him. "What's the matter?"

"The truck quit," he drawled. "I got under the hood and fooled around with everything I could think of, but she just won't go. I figured I'd just wait here until an angel of mercy came along."

"I've always wanted to be an angel," Stacy said. "Hop in the back, and I'll give you a lift."

"Thanks, but I'm too dirty to ride in the car," he said. "I would appreciate it if you'd stop by or call someone at the Broussards' and let them know I'm stranded out here."

Stacy knew all the families in Summerdale, and she recognized the name immediately. The Broussards operated a dairy farm not far from her uncle's. "Don't be silly," she said. "They've started their afternoon milking by now. It could be hours before anyone gets back out here to pick you up."

"Yeah, but I'd hate to mess up your car," he said.

"Believe me, it's seen worse," she assured him.

He gave in and opened the back door. While he folded his long frame into the back seat, Stacy made the introductions. "Drew Riley, my mother, Mrs. Diane Blair, and Joni Bothel, a friend from my old boarding school in Philadelphia."

"It's nice to meet you," Drew said, a gleam of interest in his gray eyes as he smiled at Joni. "Something tells me you've never been to Summerdale before."

"How did you know?" Joni asked.

"I would have remembered," he said.

"The only other time I was in the South was when I went to Miami with my parents a couple of years ago," Joni said.

Drew chuckled. "Miami is as much like Summerdale as . . ."

When Drew hesitated, Mrs. Blair suggested, "Paris is Philadelphia."

"Thanks," Drew said. "About halfway into that remark, I realized I didn't have a finish. I've been to Miami, but I've never lived anywhere except around here."

"Well, I have, and suddenly it's all coming back to me. I'm just remembering why I left," Diane murmured.

"Why did you want me to call the Broussards?" Stacy asked Drew. "Shouldn't I have called your mother or your uncle?"

"I'm working for Mr. Broussard. It's a better job than bagging groceries at the A&P."

Thinking of the Summerdale girl a year behind her in school, Stacy asked, "Which Broussard are you working for? Andrea's father or her brother?"

"Her father," Drew said. "Her brother may be married, but I don't call him *Mr.* Broussard."

"No, I guess not," Stacy said. "By the way, did you know that Andrea's other brother is getting married, too?"

"You mean Gary? Yeah, her little sister told me he was giving Amy Woodfin a ring at Christmas, but I thought it was a secret."

"I heard it from Tricia Allen," Stacy said.

"Finally—a name I recognize," Joni said. "Isn't Tricia your best friend in Summerdale?"

"Yes, and I'm sorry," Stacy said. "I forgot you don't know any of these people. I guess I'm just getting used to everyone knowing everyone else."

"Around here, you're considered a visitor unless people can trace your family back for two or three generations."

"Stacy, where does that leave you?" Joni asked.

"Oh, Stacy's already in," Drew said. "Whenever her name comes up, someone says, 'You know her—she's Sara Colby's niece. Her grandparents were the Webbs who lived right here in Summerdale.'"

Mrs. Blair nodded. "I haven't heard them, but I know exactly what comes next. 'Stacy's mother is Diane, Sara's older sister. You remember her, don't you? She married that man from Pennsylvania,'" Mrs. Blair said with a perfect imitation of the drawl.

Stacy and Drew were laughing uproariously, but Joni stared at them.

"You're kidding, right?" she asked.

"No, I promise, that's exactly what they say," Stacy said. "At first, I'd get lost when someone started discussing family histories, but now I can rattle them off like anyone else. Whenever I'm going to talk about anyone from school, I make sure I can tell Aunt Sara and Uncle Jim who the parents are. Then they supply the grandparents, aunts and uncles."

Stacy paused and then added, "Speaking of family histories, Mom, you probably knew Drew's mother. Her name's Lucille."

"Lucille Riley...no, I don't remember..."

"She was a Mitchell before she married," Drew informed her.

"Lucille Mitchell! Why, of course I knew her," Diane said. "We grew up together right here in Summerdale. But I don't remember any Rileys. Is your father from around here?"

"No, ma'am, he's from New Mexico. As far as we know, he's back there now. We haven't heard from him in six years."

"Oh, I'm sorry," Mrs. Blair said.

"That's all right. He and Mom were divorced years ago, and we're doing fine."

Mrs. Blair turned to Stacy. "That reminds me. Have you heard from your father?"

"Every week, just like clockwork," Stacy said. "I get a letter and an allowance check. I wrote him that you were coming here for Thanksgiving, so he wants me to spend Christmas with him in Philadelphia."

"That would be good for me, too," Mrs. Blair said. "I won't have much vacation time at Christmas, but as long as you're going to be in Philadelphia, you could come over and spend a couple of days with me in Washington."

"I'd like that," Stacy said. "I'm sure we can work it out so that I can see you and Dad."

"And me, too," Joni said.

Stacy laughed. "Yes, you, too."

She turned off the main highway and slowed down near a busy dairy. "Do you want me to let you off here or at the house?"

"Here's fine," Drew said. "Mr. Broussard may have something else he wants me to break before I knock off for the night."

Joni watched until Drew disappeared into the dairy and then settled back in her seat. "I think I'm going to like Alabama," she said.

Stacy drove on to the Colbys' and turned into the driveway, automatically swerving to avoid hitting Smokey, their German shepherd. As soon as he recognized the station wagon, he stood back and wagged his tail.

Mrs. Blair and Joni weren't totally convinced that he meant no harm and waited in the car until Sara Colby and six-year-old Angie came hurrying out of the open garage.

Sara was shorter and rounder than her more sophisticated sister, but other than that, the two women were very similar with the same fragile bone structure and wide, expressive eyes.

The dog was forgotten as the two sisters greeted each other, and Stacy introduced Joni to her youngest cousin and then to her aunt.

"I appreciate you letting me visit," Joni said. "I'm so used to having Stacy at school with me, I've really missed her this year."

"We're glad to have you," Sara replied. "Stacy's friends are always welcome here. Let's get your luggage out of the car and get you settled in. I already have coffee made.''

''I can't remember the last time I was here,'' Diane said, looking around her at the fields and barns, ''but it all looks the same.''

''Not much has changed,'' her sister agreed. ''We're still at the mercy of the crops and cows. That's where Jim and the boys are now.''

''The boys? You don't mean you keep them out of school to help around the farm, do you?''

''No, things aren't that bad,'' Sara said with a laugh. ''They got home from school about fifteen minutes ago.''

''I can't wait to see them. If they've grown as much as this little one, I won't even recognize them,'' Diane said, scooping up Angie to give her a big hug.

Angie enjoyed being the center of attention and delivered her pronouncement with great flair. ''Hal and Chris are going to stay at Grandma's while you're here.''

''They aren't going to be here?'' Diane asked, taking up the last suitcase and following the others inside.

''They're just going to spend the nights with Kate,'' Sara said. For Joni's benefit, she added, ''Kate is Jim's mother, the children's grandmother. Our house only has three bedrooms, so I'm putting Stacy and Joni in the boys' room, Angie on a cot in the bedroom with me and Jim, and Diane, you'll have the girls' room.''

Stacy had started down the hall toward her cousins' room with one of Joni's suitcases, but she remembered to ask, ''Mother, what about the things you brought for me?''

Diane pointed out which suitcase was for her, and Stacy took it along to the room she was sharing with Joni. Before she could open it, Joni said, "Oh, don't open it right now. I want to see more of the farm. I especially want to meet Lane."

"All right, let's change into some grubbies," Stacy said. "I hope you remembered to bring some with you."

"As soon as mother said I could come, I went out and bought some," Joni said.

Stacy had moved some of her clothes into the room she was sharing with Joni so she pulled an old pair of Levi's and a worn sweatshirt out of her drawer and put them on before checking out her friend.

Joni had changed into a pair of wool slacks with a matching jacket, a soft wool sweater and suede boots. Her version of grubbies.

Remembering her first days on the farm and how long it had taken before she got the "right" wardrobe, Stacy didn't comment. Besides, she was anxious to get out to the barn. She hadn't seen Lane since yesterday.

Her mother and Aunt Sara were in the kitchen, drinking coffee and trying to talk in spite of frequent interruptions from Angie. Stacy picked up her keys and waited for a break in the conversation.

"Joni and I are going," she said.

"Where? And when are you getting back?" her mother asked.

"Don't worry, Mom. I'm just taking Joni to the dairy, and we'll be home in time for dinner."

"How about taking the truck instead of the car," Sara said. "Jim picked up the cleaning supplies Lane asked about yesterday. They're still in the back of the pickup."

Joni waited until they were outside to ask "Is it always that easy for you to get to drive? I have to go through a third degree before Mom will let me near the car."

"I can't take off for Sheffield or even Douglasville unless I have a good reason, or I'm running an errand for someone," Stacy said, "but right around the farm, I'm given more freedom."

"You don't know how lucky you are," Joni said.

Stacy smiled. "Oh, I think I do."

Chapter Two

Stacy urged the old pickup truck into action and drove the mile and a half to the Colby dairy. It was a long, white concrete building situated just off the highway. At one end of the dairy was a separate room for the large refrigerated tank that held the milk. The other end was connected by a series of gates to a large holding pen where the cows to be milked waited.

As soon as she parked the truck, her cousin, Hal Colby, came out of the milk room. Although he was three years younger than Stacy, Hal was a good six inches taller, and he wasn't above using his height to bully her good-naturedly whenever he could.

"It's about time you showed up," he said.

"What are you doing here?" she asked.

"Chris went to the silos with Dad, and since you weren't around, I had to help Lane. I don't mind covering for you occasionally, but I don't expect it to become a habit."

Stacy gave him a mock salute. "Yes, sir," she snapped, and before she introduced them, she added in an aside to Joni, "I should tell you that his bark is worse than his bite."

While Joni murmured something flattering to Hal, Stacy went around to the back of the pickup and let down the gate. "Do you want me to put these supplies in the storage closet?"

"Naw, I'll get them," Hal said. "Go see what you can do about putting Lane in a better mood. If I've got to work with him, the least he could do is not bite off my head."

"What's the matter with him?" Stacy asked.

"I don't know. From the way he acts, you'd think he'd rather have you helping him instead of me."

Hal started for the truck, and Stacy motioned Joni to follow her inside the barn.

There was a center aisle running the length of the room with two feeding troughs on either side. Across from them were ten stanchions to keep the cows in place while they were being milked. As soon as a cow entered the milking parlor, she was locked into place, and while she ate, her udders were cleaned and automatic milkers put in place.

It was a hot, sweaty job in summer and a cold clammy one in the winter, but it had to be done twice a day, every day.

Lane was bent over one of the milking machines, and Stacy could tell by the set of his shoulders that he was tired. Even though the afternoon sun did little to ward off the late November chill, he wasn't wearing a jacket, and when he moved the heavy milking machine closer to the cow, the heavy muscles of his arms and back were clearly defined through the thin fabric of his shirt.

His ever-present cowboy hat was pushed to the back of his head, revealing a thick crop of blond hair. As if realizing that he was being watched, he turned around. When he spotted Stacy, a warm glow lit his brilliant blue eyes.

He started toward her eagerly but checked himself when he saw the girl with her. "When'd you get back?" he asked, his voice husky with feeling.

"A little while ago," Stacy said. "Just long enough to change clothes and get over here. I brought Joni over to meet you."

Lane acknowledged the other girl with a nod. "I'd offer to shake your hand, but I'm dirty right now."

"That's all right," Joni said, giving him the full wattage of her smile. "I think I see a clean spot right here."

Taking his acceptance for granted, she put her hands on his shoulders and standing on tiptoe, kissed him lightly on the cheek.

Lane grinned. "I keep that clean just in case I meet a pretty girl," he said.

"Stacy wanted to stay at home and look at the new clothes her mother brought her, but I insisted we come over here," Joni said. "I've never been in a dairy before, so if there's anything you want me to do, you'll have to tell me."

"You don't want to get all messed up," Lane said. "Just sit and watch. Stacy can help."

Joni looked around her. "Sit? Where?"

"Come over here, and I'll help you into the window," he said. "Stacy, get her a clean towel to sit on."

Stacy handed Joni a towel and then went to check to see that all the cows had enough food. Out of the corner of her eye, she saw Lane lift Joni to the window. She expected him to join her as soon as he got Joni settled, but between chores, he seemed content to hang around Joni and explain the operation to her.

So much for worrying whether or not they would get along, Stacy thought. They were doing just fine.

Hal finished storing the extra cleaning supplies and came back to lean against the window and talk with Joni and Lane until the last cow was let into the barn to be milked.

As soon as she finished putting out the feed, Stacy left her post at the feeding trough, slapping at the feed residue clinging to her arms and the front of her jeans.

"Since Hal's here to help you clean up, I'll take Joni back to Aunt Sara's," she told Lane.

"If you insist," Joni said and then held out her arms to Lane. "Would you help me down?"

Once Joni was back on her feet, Lane fell in and followed her and Stacy back to Jim's truck.

Out of the corner of his eye, he stole a glance at Stacy. He knew she was nervous about having her mother and friend here, but he didn't know how to reassure her that everything would be all right. It was funny, too, because he couldn't remember ever being apprehensive before Stacy arrived in Summerdale. Since then, it had been a way of life.

He had been born right here in Summerdale, and by the time his parents died when he was twelve, he thought he understood pretty much what life had to offer. He wasn't disappointed or even excited, just accepting. Then, when he was nineteen, he met Stacy Blair.

Knowing that she was only there for the summer, he had tried to hold himself aloof from her, but every day, bit by bit, she had insinuated herself a little further into his life. It got so that his every conscious thought was about her. When she admitted that she felt the same way—he couldn't believe it. He was haunted by the fear that she might change her mind about staying.

Even in her old clothes, her dark brown hair tousled and a smudge of dirt on one cheek, she was still the prettiest thing he had ever seen. Just looking at her made him feel good.

Seeking some contact with her, no matter how small, he dropped his hand onto her shoulder. "I guess you'll want to stay home with your mother and friend tonight," he said.

"I really should," Stacy said. "They're only going to be here for a few days. Besides, I'll see you at lunch tomorrow."

"Lunch?"

Joni said, "It's Thanksgiving Day, remember? The Pilgrims and Indians had a big turkey dinner together."

"Oh, yeah, that's right," he said.

They had stopped beside the truck, and he brushed the spot on Stacy's cheek with the back of his closed fist. "I guess I'll see you tomorrow, then."

Once they were on their way home, Joni said, "So that was Lane."

"What did you think of him?"

"You didn't exaggerate about his appearance—big, blond and built, but he's a little...reserved, don't you think?"

Stacy smiled. If Joni had thought that was reserved, she should have met him at the beginning of last summer. "Oh, he has his moments," she said.

With Hal and Chris spending the night at their grandmother's Jim was the only male at dinner that night, and he made the most of his position. It was a warm, wonderful meal, and afterward, Sara and Diane took over the kitchen to bake pumpkin pies for the next day, and Stacy and Joni escaped to their bedroom to talk.

Joni had a lot of gossip about the girls from the boarding school she, and previously Stacy, attended in Philadelphia. Stacy hadn't thought about Brantwood since she left at the end of last year, and she had difficulty remembering some of the girls. Still, she enjoyed hearing the school news, and while Joni talked, she had a chance to see what her mother had brought her.

As usual, her mother's sense of style was as sure as ever. From her new wardrobe, Stacy chose a royal-blue skirt and matching sweater to wear to Mrs. Colby's the next day. Normally she dressed more casually, but she wanted Lane to see that she could be as fashionable as Joni.

Mrs. Colby and Lane lived in a big, old white house situated in a grove of ancient magnolias and white oaks a mile or so beyond the dairy. Lane met them at the door and ushered them inside to some of the most appealing aromas. In addition to the immediate family, Stacy, Mrs. Blair and Joni, Mrs. Colby had invited a local bachelor, an old friend of Mrs. Blair's, to the holiday meal. There was a lot of confusion, noise and hugs during the introductions and greetings.

Under the cover of the noise, Lane moved closer to Stacy. "I missed you last night," he said softly.

"Really? Why?"

"That's a silly question," he said. "You know why."

Stacy blushed. "Yes, but we don't usually see each other on Wednesday nights," she said.

"True, but knowing you didn't have school today, and we could have been together made it different."

"We're together now," she said.

Lane grinned. "Yeah, but what I had in mind didn't include a roomful of people."

"Lane!" she admonished, her eyes darting around the room.

He chuckled. "No one else heard me, but what do you think they'd do if I grabbed you and kissed you right here?"

"You wouldn't—would you?"

"If I don't get to see you alone soon, I might," he threatened, only half joking.

"If you're going to milk this afternoon, I'll see if I can come help you."

"If you'll come, I'll be there," he said. "But what about later tonight?"

"I don't know. Let me talk to Mom and Joni and see if..."

Lane started to pull away, and she added, "It's just for a few more days, and I really want them to have a good time. It's important to me."

"What about me?" he asked.

"You're important, too, but... can't we talk about this at the barn this afternoon?"

"Talk about what?" Joni asked, joining them.

Before Stacy could reply, Mrs. Colby ordered everyone to continue visiting in the living room while she and Sara finished the last-minute preparations for dinner.

Stacy started to follow Lane, but Mrs. Colby stopped her. "Stacy, since you know where the good dishes are, you can set the table. And get Angie to help you. It's high time she learned how to do it right."

Stacy wanted a few more minutes with Lane, but she didn't know anyone who had ever ignored Mrs. Colby and lived to talk about it. Brusque and to the point, Mrs. Kate, as she was known around Summerdale, was an expert at getting things done her way.

While she worked, Stacy could hear Joni's animated voice describing to Lane how the girls in the dorm sneaked into one another's rooms and short-sheeted the beds. It wasn't long before Joni had charmed him out of his bad mood and his hearty chuckle joined her light giggle.

Stacy knew Joni wasn't just trying to be a good guest. Joni liked to flirt, and she never wasted an opportunity to practice. Pulling her eyes away from them, she encountered her mother's cool stare.

Stacy lowered her eyes and went back to her job. When lunch was finally announced, Mrs. Blair took the seat beside Stacy, effectively cutting Lane off. Stacy wasn't surprised that Joni sat beside him. Unfortunately she couldn't do anything about that. She could only handle one problem at a time.

Mrs. Kate, with some help from her mother and Aunt Sara, had prepared an honest-to-goodness banquet. In addition to the turkey and stuffing, there were all kinds of vegetables, casseroles, fruit salads, and homemade breads and pies. Conversation was light and lively, and even after they had all eaten more than they should have, no one was in any hurry to leave the table.

As soon as they could move, the men began making noises about a football game on television, and the women started gathering the dirty dishes.

"Diane, you and Joni don't have to help," Mrs. Kate said. "You're company."

"Thank you, Mrs. Kate, I would like to walk around outside," Mrs. Blair said. She looked around the room before settling on Lane. "Would you show me around?"

"Yes, ma'am, I'd be glad to," he said. "We could walk out to the dairy if you want to."

Once they were outside, Diane pulled back. "That's really not necessary. I've seen the dairy. I just wanted to come out here so that we could talk."

Lane wasn't really surprised. Every time he'd looked at Stacy, he'd felt Mrs. Blair's eyes on him. "About what?" he asked.

"Well, you and Stacy are...what's the current phrase for seeing each other?"

He shrugged. "'Seeing each other' will do."

"And neither one of you is seeing anyone else?"

"Does that bother you?"

"Not because I have any objections to you," she said hurriedly, "but naturally, I'm concerned about Stacy. She was raised with a completely different lifestyle, and I have to make sure that she's not prolonging her stay here just to keep from hurting you."

Lane didn't move. He couldn't. "Stacy wants to leave?" he asked quietly.

"No, I didn't say that—not exactly, anyway. She's been having so much fun with Joni, catching up on all the news and gossip from school and their different clubs, I haven't had a chance to talk to her myself. I thought I should find out what was going on between you two before I tried to advise her."

Lane took a deep, uneven breath. "Mrs. Blair, Stacy's free to leave whenever she wants to. I won't stand in her way."

Diane smiled. "Thank you, Lane. That's all I wanted to hear."

Her mission accomplished, Diane went back inside, but Lane didn't follow. As much as he wanted Stacy to convince him that she had no intention of leaving, he couldn't bear to face her right now. He'd wait until she came out to the barn.

Since it was too early to go to the dairy, he went out to the stables instead. Saddling his horse, he rode over the farm and back, pushing his horse until they were both exhausted.

He got back to the dairy before it was time to start milking and used the extra time to wash down the equipment and get everything ready so that he would have more time with Stacy once she got there. When he finally heard a truck drive up, Lane told himself that he would wait and let her come to him, but he was already on his way to the door.

Instead of Stacy, he saw Hal headed toward him.

"Where's Stacy?" he asked.

"She and Joni went with Mama and Aunt Diane to visit some friends in Douglasville."

"What time did they say they would get back?"

"I don't know. They took Angie with them, too, and Mama said for me and Chris to have dinner with Grandma. She said she'd see us tomorrow."

"Did Stacy say anything?"

"Not to me," Hal said.

He went inside and began filling the feed troughs. When he finished, he looked up, and Lane hadn't moved from the barn door. "Hey, Lane," he called. "Are you ready to let the cows in?"

Lane pushed away from the door frame, scowling. "I've been ready for the past hour. If you'd been here on time, we could have been through with the first bunch by now," he said harshly.

Lane opened the gate to the holding pen, and as the cows came to the feed trough, Hal was there to lock them in place. He was at the barn on time, in fact, he was a few minutes early. He didn't, however, correct his cousin.

Hal had been so young when Lane's parents died in the car accident, he could hardly remember them, but he couldn't imagine life without Lane. In many ways, Lane was more like a big brother than a cousin. He couldn't tolerate sloppy work or irresponsibility and his highest praise could be a silent nod of approval, but he was always there whenever anyone needed him. And if he needed to blow off a little steam occasionally, it was all right with Hal.

Fortunately Hal didn't need any help keeping up. Lane went through the motions, doing what had to be done without words or wasted motions. When they finished, they cleaned up the barn and took the truck back to their grandmother's house. Mrs. Kate and Chris were already waiting supper for them.

"Any calls?" Lane asked as soon as he walked in.

"No," his grandmother said, "but Stacy left you a note. I put it under the telephone in the hall."

Trying not to hurry, Lane went to get the note. It was a simple message written in three lines.

Please understand. Mom wants to go to see some of her old friends, so I'm not sure when I'll get back. See you tomorrow.
Stacy

After reading it over a couple more times, he wadded it up and stuck it into his pocket. He understood all right. Her mother wanted to see her old friends. Joni was Stacy's old friend. Together they had a past—a history he didn't know anything about.

On his way back through the kitchen, Mrs. Kate stopped him. "We got tired of waiting, so I went ahead and gave the boys their supper. Where are you going?"

"Out," he said, and then added, "I'm not hungry, Grandma."

"Are you going to see Stacy?" Mrs. Kate asked. "If you are, you can take some of these leftovers to Sara."

"I'm not headed that way. If Stacy calls while I'm out, tell her...never mind, she won't call," he added, closing the door quickly behind him.

Chapter Three

When Stacy got up the next morning, her aunt was alone in the kitchen. The doors and windows were closed against the morning chill, but Stacy could hear the calves bawling. "Haven't they been fed yet?" she asked.

"No, but one of the boys will be here to take care of them pretty soon," Sara said. "You have company. You don't have to help this weekend."

Stacy was already heading for the door. "That's all right. I'll be through before Joni ever gets up."

On her way to the shed to mix up the powdered milk for the ten or so calves that they were raising on bottles, Stacy met Chris on his way home from his grandmother's.

"I told Lane you'd feed the calves for us, but he made me come check on them anyway," Chris said.

When she first came to Summerdale, Stacy had been embarrassed to have her ten-year-old cousin showing her around the farm and teaching her how to do some of the chores. But in spite of his age, Chris was the logical choice. Because he was only ten, he had more free time than his brother or father, and the chores he did, although necessary, didn't require a lot of strength or expertise.

It was a messy job, but she had learned to feed the calves all by herself, she knew enough to be good help at the dairy, and because she had her driver's license, she could run errands for her uncle and Lane, freeing them for more important things.

"If you need to do something else," she told Chris, "I can handle the calves."

"That's all right. I'm here now," Chris said. "I'll help."

Working together made the job go much faster, and after they finished, Stacy drove Chris over to meet his father at the silos.

On the way, she asked him, "Did you help Lane at the dairy yesterday afternoon?"

"Uh-uh, Hal did. Why?"

"I just wondered if Lane said anything about me not being there," Stacy said. "He wasn't angry or upset about anything last night, was he?"

"I don't know. He went out, and I was in bed before he came home. Why? Did y'all have a fight?"

"No, of course not. Things are just a little crazy with Mom and Joni here. Everything will be back to normal in a few days," she said, with more conviction than she felt.

By the time Stacy got back home, her mother was up. Stacy washed up and joined her and Angie at the table.

"Lane called while you were gone," Aunt Sara said. "He said to tell you that Jim was milking this evening, so he was free if you wanted to do something."

Stacy relaxed a little. Obviously he wasn't too upset. "I thought about calling Tricia Allen and asking her if she and her boyfriend would like to meet us at Drury's tonight," Stacy said.

"Drury's?" Mrs. Blair asked and then turned to her sister. "She's not talking about that beer joint that used to be here when we were growing up, is she?"

"The very same," Aunt Sara replied. "Some things never change."

"Only now it's called a club," Stacy said.

"Well you can't go there," her mother protested. "You're only seventeen."

"Mom, don't worry. They don't serve drinks to minors. They just let us come over and dance as long as we don't cause any trouble. Besides, everyone around here knows us. It's not as though we'd try to get away with a fake identification or anything."

"There haven't been any problems," Aunt Sara assured her sister.

Her mother still didn't look very happy, but she didn't voice any more objections, so Stacy called Tricia as soon as she finished breakfast.

Tricia was the first girl her own age that Stacy met when she came to Summerdale, and they had become good friends almost immediately. Tall, slim and blond, with a light sprinkle of freckles across her nose, Tricia Allen fit the classic description of the all-American girl. She could get along with everyone, and it was her personality as much as her looks that made her popular with teenagers and adults alike. In school, she was head cheerleader, Key Club sweetheart and class secretary. Everyone confided in Tricia, and Stacy counted herself lucky that she was the one in whom Tricia confided.

"How was your Thanksgiving?" Stacy asked when Tricia came on the telephone.

"Fantastic," Tricia said. She had had a crush on a local boy, Chuck Hastings, for years and had finally started dating him last summer. He was in college, though, and this was his first visit home since school started.

"Chuck called me as soon as he got home Wednesday night and invited me to have Thanksgiving dinner with his family. What about you? Did your mother and friend from Philadelphia get there? Is everything going all right?"

"I'll fill you in on that later," Stacy said. "I was calling to see if you and Chuck were doing anything special tonight, or if you wanted to meet us at Drury's. You could meet Joni, and it would give Lane and Chuck a chance to see each other."

"Sounds like fun," Tricia agreed. "I'll talk to Chuck, and if you don't hear from me, we'll see you there. Are you going to get a date for Joni?"

"I was thinking about Drew Riley. We picked him up the other day on the shortcut in from Sheffield, and he seemed interested in Joni."

"Drew Riley's interested in girls, period," Tricia said. "Have you already called him?"

"No, he said he was working for Andrea Broussard's father, so I thought Joni and I might just go over there and ask him in person."

"Good luck," Tricia said.

"Why? Is there a problem?"

"Rumor has it that he doesn't work for Mr. Broussard just for the money. I think he likes Andrea."

"Oh? I didn't know that," Stacy said.

"I didn't say Andrea liked him. She probably just keeps him around in case she gets bored. Go ahead and check with him. If he can't go, for whatever reason, call me back. Maybe we can fix Joni up with Chuck's brother."

"We'll ride over there as soon as Joni gets up."

"Joni's up," Joni said, coming into the kitchen. "Where are we going? Shopping?"

"You might say that," Stacy said. "Do you want to eat breakfast before we go?"

Joni shook her head. "Just some juice. I have to be really awake before I can eat anything. If I remember correctly, you used to be the same way."

"I still am," Stacy said, "but I've been up for hours. Go ahead and have your juice. I'll go saddle some horses, and we'll ride over, if that's all right with you?"

"As long as you have a gentle horse that won't throw me," Joni said.

For Joni, Stacy chose Nellie, the old family pet that even Angie had outgrown. She led her over to the mounting block, adjusted the stirrups and showed Joni how to hold the reins with one hand and hold onto the saddle horn with the other. Even with Stacy's constant assurances, Joni was too nervous to enjoy the short ride over to the Broussards' farm.

Since they were on horseback, Stacy passed the front drive and went around to the back of the house. They dismounted and tied their horses to the fence.

Yvette, the youngest Broussard and Andrea's little sister, came out to meet them.

"Is it all right if we leave our horses here?" Stacy asked.

"Sure," Yvette said. "Unless you want me to put them in the corral."

"Thanks, but we won't be here that long," Stacy said. "We just came to see Drew. Is he around?"

"Do you have something from Mr. Colby? I mean, did your uncle send you . . . ?"

"Oh, no. It's nothing like that," Stacy said. "It's personal. Your father won't mind if we talk to him, will he?"

Yvette shook her head and motioned for them to follow her. "Drew's cleaning out the stables. I think he can probably handle that and a conversation at the same time."

Coming out of the bright sunlight, they paused a minute at the stable door for their eyes to become accustomed to the dusty, darkened shadows of the interior. Drew was busy raking dirty straw out of the stalls into the center aisle, but he seemed happy enough to take a break when he saw them.

"I know," he said, grinning at them. "You're taking your friend around to show her what kind of chores we do on a farm."

"Actually I'm more interested in the farm boys than their chores," Joni said, letting a suggestive smile play around the corners of her mouth.

"And I'm fast developing an interest in big-city girls," Drew said.

"Excuse me," Stacy said quickly, "but I don't think there's going to be a better time to ask you if you'd like to go to Drury's with us tonight."

"Us?" Drew asked.

"Well, I'm going with Lane, and we'll meet Tricia Allen and Chuck Hastings there."

"And I'd be her date?"

"If you don't mind," Joni said, batting her lashes at him. "I'm a stranger in town, and you know how lonely that can be."

"I can't imagine you ever being lonely," Drew said, "but I'd be happy to go with you."

"I'm not sure why I even bothered to come," Stacy murmured to Yvette before saying aloud, "I'll let Lane know to pick you up before he comes over tonight. Where will you be? Here or at your uncle's?"

"I'll have to get cleaned up before I go. Tell him to pick me up at Uncle Mike's."

Stacy and Joni were headed back toward their horses with Yvette when they saw Andrea coming toward them.

Andrea Broussard didn't have Joni's polish or Tricia's personality, but she didn't need them. In addition to an eye-catching figure, she had long ash-blond hair, hazel eyes with incredibly long lashes and a true peaches-and-cream complexion.

"Good morning," she called, her soft Southern drawl completing the picture she made. "I saw the horses and thought maybe Hal and Chris had come by to see Yvette."

"Oh sure," Yvette said. "That's why you got all dolled up and put on that tight sweater."

"Well, I have to admit I wouldn't have been disappointed if I'd run into Lane out here," Andrea said.

"We just stopped by to see Drew," Stacy said and then remembered to make the introductions. "Andrea Broussard, a friend of mine from Philadelphia, Joni Bothel."

"Are you out taking in some of the local color?" Andrea asked.

"Actually she's out making dates with some of the local boys," Yvette said, delighting in needling her older sister.

Andrea didn't try to hide her surprise. "Drew? What made you think of him?"

"Joni met him Wednesday," Stacy said.

"I would have thought you'd want someone a little more... uh, worldly," Andrea suggested.

"Oh, I don't know. I think Drew's cute," Joni said.

"Where are y'all going?"

"Drury's," Stacy said.

"Maybe I'll see you there."

Stacy unhitched their horses, and after a few unsuccessful attempts, she finally got Joni back into the saddle, and they started home.

"I don't know why people think Southerners are slow," Joni said. "That child is definitely advanced for her age."

"And it happened so fast," Stacy said. "Last summer she was just another kid playing around the swimming pool at the community center, but when I got back from spending a few weeks with Mom and Dad at the end of August, she had blossomed."

"I mean to tell you she's blossomed," Joni said. "She looks like she could give me lessons in how to flirt, and I'm pretty good, if I do say so myself."

"Really?" Stacy pretended to be surprised. "Why, I'd never know it."

"You don't really mind me flirting with Lane, do you? If you don't think you can trust him, I could let up some."

Stacy didn't want Joni to think she didn't trust Lane, but she didn't want to hold him up as a challenge, either. "Joni, do whatever you feel like doing," she said.

Both Joni and Stacy dressed carefully for their dates that night. Joni wanted to show the local girls a thing or two about fashion and style, and Stacy was looking forward to spending some time with Lane. She had to make sure he understood why she hadn't met him at the barn as they had planned.

At the last minute, her mother had made it clear that she expected Stacy to go visiting with her. Not wanting her mother to think that Lane was monopolizing all of her time, Stacy had given in without a complaint. Now she pulled a curl away from her face and tried to keep it in place with a spritz of hair spray. As far as she was concerned, Lane didn't monopolize enough of her time—just all of her thoughts.

Lane and Drew arrived promptly at eight. After spending a few minutes talking to Uncle Jim and Aunt Sara, and reassuring Stacy's mother that they would leave Drury's at the first sign of any trouble, they went out to Lane's car.

"I see you got my message," Stacy said.

"Which message is that?" Lane asked. "You've been leaving a lot of them the past few days."

"I was talking about picking up Drew tonight. What are you talking about?"

"The note Grandma gave me when I got home from the barn last night."

"I'm sorry about that, but I didn't know what else to do," Stacy said. "You took off right after lunch, and no one knew where you were."

Lane and Stacy weren't talking very loud, but their voices carried to the back seat, and Joni unabashedly joined their conversation. "I want to make sure I don't get blamed for what happened," she said. "I told them I'd rather stay at the dairy with you."

What Joni had really said was that she would rather go somewhere with Lane, but Stacy didn't correct her in front of everyone.

"I wasn't going to blame anyone," Stacy told her. "Mom and Aunt Sara were visiting and time just got away from us."

"Not really," Joni said. "You told that one lady that you'd rather be at her house than at the barn."

"I was trapped," Stacy said. "Mrs. Cobb asked if we could stay for a piece of cake, and I told her I should be at the barn. Mom made a joke about whether I'd rather be there having cake with them or working at the barn, and I couldn't tell that sweet old lady that I preferred work to her cooking...could I?"

Lane didn't comment, and Stacy turned away. As if unaware of the tension in the front seat, Joni kept up a flow of amusing talk until they arrived at Drury's.

Located far from everything and unadorned except for a single string of colored lights, the small tavern looked almost sinister. Joni made several observations about what could happen to people who entered such places, but she followed them inside eagerly.

In contrast to the forbidding exterior, the interior was clean, warm and glowing with subdued lights. Beyond a long bar crowded with stools, tables were set up around a small dance floor. The band was already playing, and with the sound bouncing off the walls, it was impossible to talk in normal tones.

Since it was too early for the serious party goers to be out in force, the room wasn't very crowded. Lane spotted Tricia and Chuck across the room and motioned for the others to follow him. The band ended its number and didn't start the next one until Stacy had introduced Joni, and Drew asked everyone what they wanted to drink.

As soon as Drew left to go get their order, Joni said, "Oh, I just love to dance to that song. Lane, will you dance with me?"

Lane let himself be pulled onto the floor. It was a moderately fast song, and as Stacy watched Joni and Lane move across the floor, threading their way through the other dancers, she could see the animation on their faces. Lane hadn't smiled at her once all evening, she thought sadly.

Drew returned with their Cokes before Joni and Lane came back to the table. Joni gulped her drink gratefully and said, "That was fun. The dances we have at school are always so brightly lit, no one wants to be the first couple on the floor. We all hold back, waiting for someone else to go first, and miss half of the song."

"It's the same way at our high school," Tricia admitted.

"Stacy, remember the time we were going to throw a few of the light switches and ended up putting out all the lights on campus?" Joni asked.

"Stacy did that?" Tricia asked. "I can't believe it."

"I know what you mean," Joni said. "But this girl, the one who's with us tonight, is not the same person who went to Brantwood with me. Did she ever tell you what we used to do in parking lots? We'd find the hottest looking cars there and put notes on the windshields. One time..."

Stacy broke in quickly, "Joni, don't you want to dance again?"

Joni grinned. "I think my friend has gone shy, but that's all right, I haven't. Come on, Drew, let's dance."

Lane and Chuck hadn't seen each other in some time, and they were doing their best to talk over the noise of the band, but after a few casual remarks, Tricia and Stacy gave up and just watched the other dancers. Stacy noticed that while he talked, Chuck kept a tight hold on Tricia's hand. Lane kept both of his hands wrapped around his drink.

Joni got Lane to dance with her again, and Drew, and even Chuck. Tricia danced with Drew and Lane, and Stacy danced with Drew and Chuck. Finally Lane led her onto the floor.

Stacy's heart beat faster, but Lane didn't say a word during the entire dance, and instead of cuddling her close, he held her as if she were a stranger. Walking back to their table, she tried to tease him out of his somber mood. "I didn't think you were going to dance with me at all," she said.

"Why? Just because you stood me up yesterday?"

"Lane, I didn't stand you up. I just didn't get to the dairy. It's not exactly the same thing."

"Maybe not to someone who expects all her dates to drive fancy cars and take her to dances and dinner theaters," Lane said. "Some people think who they are with is more important than where they go," he said.

"That's not fair," she protested.

Tricia and Chuck hadn't made it back to the table, but Joni and Drew were there. Instead of sitting down, Lane pulled out Stacy's chair for her and turned to Joni. "Come on, one more dance," he said. "I think I'm just getting the hang of that new step you were trying to teach me."

Joni readily agreed, and on their way back to the floor, they passed Chuck and Tricia.

"Excuse me, but was that really Lane Colby?" Chuck asked.

"And my date," Drew said.

Chuck shook his head. "I've never seen him dance so much in one evening. Maybe I should dance with your friend again. She's obviously—"

Tricia poked him in the ribs, cutting off the rest of his sentence. "I think it's time for us to go," she said. "Stacy, are y'all going to stay much longer?"

"No, we'll probably leave when Joni and Lane finish their dance," Stacy said. "We'll see you later."

Joni wasn't ready for the evening to end, and she protested, "But it's still early."

"Yeah, but Stacy's right. It's a good idea to leave before this place gets rowdy," Lane said.

Drew and Joni talked softly all the way home, but Lane and Stacy didn't say anything that wasn't absolutely necessary. When they stopped at Drew's uncle's house, Joni made a big fuss about being a courteous date and seeing Drew to his door.

It was the first time Lane and Stacy had been alone in over a week, but Lane was determined to remain as aloof and detached as Stacy was. His determination lasted until Joni and Drew disappeared into the shadows of Drew's front door.

He couldn't help himself. She was here now, just inches away. He'd argue with her later, when they had more time to work things out. Sliding his hand along the back of the seat, he turned to pull her into his arms, but Stacy pushed him away.

"Lane, wait. We have to talk!"

"Later," he murmured.

"No, now. You can't ignore me all evening, and then—" She broke off as Joni came back to the car.

Lane gripped the steering wheel with both hands, and driving away, he clenched his teeth so fiercely that the cords of his neck stood out. No one spoke, and as soon as they stopped at Stacy's aunt's, Joni got out and Stacy followed.

At the last minute, she stopped and turned around. "You know, you've been angry with me for not meeting you yesterday, but Chris told me you weren't even home last night."

"That's the point. Chris had to tell you. You didn't even bother to call and find out for yourself."

Chapter Four

After a fitful night, Stacy overslept and got up the next morning feeling out of sorts. Stiff and groggy, she made her way to the kitchen where her mother and Aunt Sara were listening to Chris describe the trouble he had moving some of the calves.

Stacy poured herself a cup of coffee and sat down beside her mother.

"Are you all right?" Mrs. Blair asked, running her hand over Stacy's forehead.

"I'm not sick," Stacy said. "I just don't like sleeping so late."

"I told them," Chris said. "I wanted to wake you up to help me, but they wouldn't let me."

Stacy gave him a dry smile. "You're so kind."

"What have you planned for today?" her mother asked.

"Nothing yet. Why?"

"I thought you and I might ride over to the house."

Stacy knew exactly which house her mother meant. *Her* house. It had been her mother and Aunt Sara's childhood home, but having left their land to Aunt Sara's children, her grandparents willed their house to Stacy.

"What about Joni?" Stacy asked. "Should I wake her or..."

"That's all right. You two go ahead. I'll take care of Joni when she gets up," Aunt Sara said.

"Thanks," Stacy replied. "Mom, would you like me to saddle us some horses?"

"No, thank you," she said firmly. "It's been too long since I've done any horseback riding. I think we should take the car instead."

Once they were outside, Mrs. Blair hesitated. "You know, this station wagon seems so large for just the two of us. Maybe we should use the truck instead."

"No, it's better this way," Stacy said. "We really should leave the truck in case Uncle Jim or Lane need it."

"Sometimes it's hard for me to believe that I was the one who grew up on a farm. You seem more at home here than I ever was."

"Maybe it's because I want to belong, and you couldn't wait to get away," Stacy said.

Stacy's house wasn't far from her aunt's, so it wasn't long before they were turning into the driveway. The house had been recently painted, the grass was cut and the hedges neatly trimmed.

"I almost expect to see Mother coming to the door to invite us in for pie and coffee," Mrs. Blair said.

"I can't manage the pie, but we do have water and a small gas stove. I can make us some instant coffee,"

Stacy suggested. "I keep some here so that I can have a cup whenever I come by to check on things."

While Stacy went to the kitchen and put some water on to boil, her mother wandered through the house, touching the furniture, looking through the windows, and remembering. Finally she joined Stacy on the porch.

There was a cup of coffee waiting for her on a tray, and Stacy was sitting on the swing, sipping hers as she stared off at the sky.

"Looking at you, I would never guess that you had known any other kind of life except this," her mother said wryly.

Stacy smiled. "I was just thinking about what it must have been like for you and Aunt Sara growing up here."

"It was wonderful and simple and, for me, stifling. Sara always had Jim, so she didn't feel the same way."

"How old were they when they first started dating?" Stacy asked.

"Oh, heavens, I can't remember when Jim Colby wasn't coming around," her mother said with a laugh. "At first, he came on his bicycle, and then his horse, and finally in a truck or car. I remember Dad used to say that Jim was around so much he didn't even have to pay a hired hand to help out."

"What about you? Were any of the local men your boyfriends?"

"Oh, I dated a number of them, but I was never serious. I think I always knew that I wouldn't stay here permanently. I guess I thought you might feel the same way."

"Are you having second thoughts about letting me live with Aunt Sara and finish school in Douglasville?" Stacy asked.

"No, not really," Mrs. Blair said. "Sara and Jim seem genuinely happy to have you, and you've certainly made yourself at home. Only...I don't expect you to end your education this year. There's still college."

"I haven't forgotten, but there are colleges in Alabama."

"Our arrangement was for you to graduate from high school here and then return east for college."

"Would you object if I wanted to stay here?"

Mrs. Blair paused and took a sip of coffee. "Stacy, I want you to be able to do all the things I never had a chance to do."

"What about what I want to do?"

"Does this change of heart have anything to do with Lane?"

"I haven't kept it a secret from you about the way I feel about Lane," Stacy said.

"Yes, I know. You're in love with him, or at least you think you are." Before Stacy could protest, her mother added, "Sometimes it's possible to be in love with the idea of being in love."

"And you think that's what's happened to me?"

"I think it's possible. Lane is a very nice-looking young man, and I can see that he would be an attractive target to a young girl. Especially one who was as confused and hurt as you were when you first came here."

"I'm not confused anymore," Stacy said, "And even if Lane and I weren't...involved, I'd still want to live here."

"Do you remember how miserable you were when you first came here?" her mother asked. "You begged me to send for you. How do you know you won't change your mind again?"

"It's not the same," Stacy protested. "I didn't know anyone in Summerdale then, and I was upset about your divorce. It's different now."

"I know. For one thing, you've had a chance to get to know your aunt and uncle, and you've seen how happy they are. I just want you to understand that it doesn't work out that way for everyone."

"You think I'm just trying to copy Aunt Sara? Marry a Colby and live happily ever after in Summerdale?"

"Sara is a powerful role model," her mother said.

Stacy knew that was true. Watching Aunt Sara, she had daydreamed about living on a farm in Summerdale with her husband and their three happy children. And, of course, in her dreams the husband was always Lane.

Mrs. Blair interrupted her thoughts. "This was the perfect place for you to be cared for and comforted while your father and I were going through our divorce, but I don't want you to stay here because it's safe. The whole world is just starting to open up for you. Don't limit your choices before you've had a chance to see what's out there."

"Mom, I—Lane and I haven't made any decisions that would affect our future. Not yet, anyway."

"I know. I've already talked to Lane. I think he understands better than you how different you two are. He made it clear that it was all right with him if you wanted to leave."

Stacy felt as if all the oxygen had been sucked out of the air or that she had forgotten how to breathe. Lane said that? When? He hadn't even mentioned a conversation with her mother!

As soon as she could breathe normally, Stacy stood up and began clearing away the coffee cups. She didn't want this conversation to go any further until she had a chance to talk to Lane.

"We'd better get back to Aunt Sara's," she said. "Joni must be up by now and wondering what happened to me."

Stacy was only half right. Joni was up, but by the time Stacy and her mother returned, she was gone.

"Lane stopped by on his way to the stockyards, and Joni went with him," Aunt Sara said.

"Did he say what time they'd get back?" Stacy asked.

"No, but he was just delivering some of our calves to the sale," Aunt Sara said. "They shouldn't be too long."

"Then I guess I'll go straighten our room. I don't want Hal and Chris yelling at me for contaminating their things with *girl's stuff*."

"When you finish in there, would you mind vacuuming the living room?" her aunt asked. "Kate and Lane are coming for dinner and bringing the boys. Since it's Joni and Diane's last night, I wanted to make something special."

With the vacuum cleaner running, Stacy didn't hear Lane's truck or realize that Joni had returned until she felt a tap on her shoulder. She switched the machine off as she turned around.

"How did you like the stockyard?" she asked.

"I didn't," Joni said with a delicate shudder.

"Really? I do," Stacy said. "It's noisy and smelly, but there's always so much going on."

"Yes, but did you know they're selling those calves to be killed?"

"Of course. Where do you think you get hamburgers and filets mignons?"

"Frankly I try not to think about it at all. I'd rather not get personally involved."

"Riding to the stockyard is hardly getting involved," Stacy said dryly.

"I did enjoy the ride," Joni admitted. "After we got there, some guys started giving me the eye, but Lane let them know I was with him."

"Who were they?" Stacy asked.

"I don't know. Some unkempt-looking characters. Lane just glared at them, and they left me alone," Joni said. "It made me feel sort of safe and protected. Believe me, I let Lane know I appreciated it."

"Well, I'm through here," Stacy said, abruptly picking up the vacuum cleaner and cutting off Joni's words. She stored the vacuum cleaner away and asked, "What would you like to do now?"

"Well, I've seen the farm, the dairy and the stockyards," Joni said. "Isn't there something else we can do? Shopping or just go somewhere and have a Coke?"

"There's nothing like that in Summerdale, but we could go into Douglasville to the Dairy Queen," Stacy said. "I'll clear it with Aunt Sara and call Tricia. If she's not busy with Chuck—"

Joni interrupted her. "Couldn't we just go by ourselves? I'd like to see if I can find the real Stacy Blair."

Stacy waited until they were in the car on their way to Douglasville before asking, "Do you really think I've changed that much?"

"Oh, Stace, you've got to be kidding!" Joni laughed. "You haven't talked about anything except the farm or the local yokels since I've been here. In case you've forgotten, there's a whole world out there—department stores, rock concerts, theaters with first-run movies, and yes, even French restaurants!"

"I beg your pardon, but there's a French restaurant in Sheffield," Stacy said.

"Is it any good?"

"I don't know. I've never been to it."

"I rest my case," Joni said dryly.

"I have been thinking about how gorgeous the fall leaves are at this time of year," Stacy admitted. "And I do miss the department stores. Aunt Sara and I went shopping a couple of weeks ago, and it made me realize what a problem I was going to have filling my Christmas shopping list."

"See? I knew you were in there somewhere," Joni said.

For the rest of the day, Stacy made a conscious effort to keep the conversation centered around Brantwood, people they knew from Philadelphia, and the new trendy shops that Joni described.

"It's too bad that Douglasville doesn't have any large department stores. We could go to one of their cosmetic counters and have a make-over done on you," Joni said. "If you don't mind me saying so, your makeup is beginning to look a little dated."

It was on the tip of Stacy's tongue to tell Joni that she didn't need a makeover, that she was happy just the way she was, but she caught herself. Surely that couldn't be the problem. Was Lane bored with her because she wasn't as glamorous as her friend? She pushed the thought aside and changed the subject.

"I can't believe that this is our last year of high school," she said. "Do you have any idea what you're going to study in college? Or what you'll be doing ten years from now?"

"I know what kind of life I want, I'm just not sure which path I'm going to take to get there."

"Well, that still makes you one step ahead of me," Stacy said.

"I want to be in a position to make decisions that really matter, something exciting and maybe even high-pressured. Maybe I could be a buyer for a department store—I like things having to do with fashions and clothes. I just know I don't want to be anything safe like a secretary or nurse or teacher."

"What about marriage? Do you think about that?"

"Sure, sometimes. But it's not something you plan your whole life around. I mean, we have to plan for our future because we're all going to grow up whether we want to or not. We may or may not get married."

"And even if we do—marriages don't always last," Stacy said.

"Yuk! How did we get so serious?" Joni asked. "Let's talk about something that's really fun, like graduation presents. Now, that's what I call planning for the future."

"What do you have in mind?"

"I was thinking that we could ask our parents to let us go to Europe after graduation."

"Alone?"

"Naturally. It wouldn't be any fun if we had to take chaperons. What do you think?"

"That we have two chances—slim and none."

"What if we asked them for permission to take the trip next year? After our freshman year in college?"

"We would have a better chance," Stacy agreed. "Plus, that would give us a whole year to plan the trip."

"And you'll sound your parents out on the idea?"

"I'll think about it," Stacy said.

They stopped at the Dairy Queen for a Coke, but except for a young mother and two noisy children, they were the only customers.

"This is what you do for excitement?" Joni asked.

"I didn't say it was exciting," Stacy said. "It's just someplace to go. I guess everyone's working or busy doing something else right now. To be honest, I think this is the first time I've been here on a Saturday afternoon."

"Christmas won't be here too soon. We've got to get you away from here for a while," Joni said.

When they returned home, Joni brought out her camera, and she and Stacy took turns taking pictures of each other around the farm.

"I took some pictures of Lane at the stockyard today," Joni said. "When I show them around school, everyone will understand why you're still here."

Her mother had said almost the same thing, Stacy thought. If she didn't know better, she'd suspect her mother put Joni up to saying something, but no, Joni had made it clear that she was impressed with Lane—if nothing else.

Not that she blamed her, Stacy thought as she changed clothes for dinner. Lane was special. If only things could be right between them again! When did he decide that he didn't care if she left? After he met Joni? When she didn't meet him Thanksgiving Day? Or had he always felt that way? She had to find a way to talk to him, and soon.

As if on cue, she heard Smokey barking.

With a final check on her appearance, she went out to join them. She had taken a cue from Joni and spent more time on her makeup, and she was wearing another one of the outfits her mother had brought her. This time it was a simple skirt and vest of bleached denim with a crisp white blouse and pair of high-heeled suede boots.

"Why are you all dressed up?" Hal asked as soon as he saw her. "Are you going somewhere?"

"Just in here to see you," she quipped.

"Aunt Diane brought her a lot of new clothes," Angie said. "And she said I could borrow them as soon as I got big enough to wear them."

"Well, tell her to keep the boots. I don't think you'll want them," Mrs. Colby said.

"Oh, no, they're classics," Joni said. "Everyone's wearing them."

"Not to get any work done," Mrs. Colby said. "They wouldn't hold up a week at the barn."

"I don't think I'll wear these to the barn. I'll keep the ones I have for that," Stacy said.

"I can't wait to get you back home," Joni told her. "Just wait until you see the new leather shop in the mall. You're going to die!"

"Stacy's not going back with you," Angie said. "She lives here now."

Stacy felt everyone looking at her, and she carefully avoided looking at anyone as she hugged Angie.

"Of course I do, but you know I'm going to visit my father at Christmas."

"And college next year," Joni added. "And Europe."

"What's this about Europe?" Mrs. Blair asked.

"Just something Stacy and I were discussing this afternoon. We've decided to go to Europe after graduation."

"Whose idea was this?" Mrs. Blair asked.

"I wanted to go this summer right after graduation, but Stacy thought we should wait until after we had finished a year of college. What do you think?"

"I think it's something we need to talk about with your parents and Stacy's father," Mrs. Blair said.

Stacy couldn't resist adding "Mom, you told me that the whole world was opening for me. I just want to go see it."

Everyone laughed, except Lane.

Under the cover of their laughter, he took a seat in the corner of the room where he could watch Stacy without being observed. College and then Europe. He'd been a fool to think she could be happy here. He had purposely taken Joni to the stockyards with him, hoping he could get her to talk about Stacy. Of course, getting Joni to talk hadn't been a problem. Still, he hadn't learned anything about Stacy that could help him now.

He didn't taste anything he ate at dinner, and as soon as he finished, he stood up. "I need to go check on one of the cows," he told Jim. "She didn't look well this afternoon, so I put her back in the holding pen. We might have to call the vet in the morning."

"Do you want me to go with you?" Jim asked.

"No, I'll take care of her," he said. "If I'm not back by the time Grandma's ready to go, let Hal drive home."

Hal had been driving the trucks and other farm equipment since he was big enough to see over the steering wheel, but he rarely drove on the highway and never at night.

Stacy knew that Lane wasn't planning to come back. She slipped outside behind him and called, "Lane, wait!"

He stopped in midstride but didn't turn around. "I really have to go, Stacy."

"I'll go with you," she said.

He turned slowly, and his blue eyes, usually so warm and tender, were cold and expressionless. "You might get your clothes dirty," he said.

"I can change," she said quickly.

He hesitated and then shook his head. "I don't think that's necessary."

Before she could reply, he ducked into his car and drove off.

Chapter Five

While Aunt Sara, Uncle Jim and Angie dressed for church the next morning, Stacy helped her mother and Joni load their suitcases into the car.

"Next time, don't wait so long to visit," Sara told her sister as they got ready to leave.

"I won't. Especially now that Stacy's here," Mrs. Blair said.

"Why don't you plan to come back for Christmas? Then we could keep Stacy, too," Sara suggested.

"I wish I could, but Stacy is supposed to spend Christmas with Warren. I'll be happy if I can work it out so that I'll be able to see her while she's there. Warren and I will probably both be here this spring for her graduation."

"Joni, you're welcome to come back anytime," Aunt Sara said. "You don't have to wait for Diane to come."

"Thank you, Mrs. Colby," Joni replied. "I had a wonderful time."

As they got into the car, Aunt Sara asked Stacy, "Are you going to be back in time to meet us at Kate's for lunch?"

"I don't think so," Stacy said. "Their plane doesn't leave until one-thirty, so we'll have lunch in Sheffield before they leave. I probably won't be home until three."

"Well, be careful and call us at home or Kate's if anything happens."

"I will," Stacy said.

She, her mother and Joni were quiet on the trip back to Sheffield and even during lunch in one of the better restaurants. Stacy wasn't really glad that they were leaving, but she was anxious for her life to get back to normal.

When they said their final goodbyes in the airport, Joni added, "When you come home at Christmas, I'll handle the entertainment. I may not be able to come up with anything as interesting as a local beer joint or a trip to a stockyard, but I'll see what I can do about arranging us some hot dates."

"Don't worry about any dates for me. I'll be happy enough to see you and Mom, and spend some time with Dad," Stacy said.

"And, in the meantime, you won't forget what we talked about?" her mother asked.

"I won't, Mom, but—"

The final boarding call came over the public address system, interrupting Stacy.

"I just want what's best for you," Mrs. Blair added hastily.

"I know," Stacy said.

She gave her mother and friend a final hug and waved until they disappeared down the passageway. With mixed emotions, she watched their plane take off.

Aunt Sara and Angie were the only ones at home when Stacy got back from the airport. Angie was happy to fill her in on everything that had happened in her absence. "Mama and I already fed the calves. Daddy and Hal are checking on some fields, and Chris is helping Lane at the dairy. He said you could help them when you got back."

"Who said that? Lane?"

"No, Chris."

Stacy hesitated. "Do you think they really need me?" she asked her aunt.

"I'm sure they can manage without you," Aunt Sara said. "Why? Is there something else you need to do?"

"Well... I do have some homework. Since we have to go back to school tomorrow, I should get started on it."

"Go ahead," Aunt Sara said. "I'll call you when it's time for dinner."

In her room, Stacy piled her books on her bed and crawled onto it with them. She had to write an essay for English and do a page of review problems for Algebra II. So far, she hadn't had any problems with her classes or her homework assignments, but she couldn't seem to concentrate.

It hadn't escaped her notice that Chris, not Lane, had suggested she come to the dairy. After last night, should she wait for Lane to come to see her? And what if her mother was right? What if she just wanted to believe she was in love with him?

Stacy waited all evening for Lane to call but the only call she got was one from her mother, letting her know that she and Joni had arrived home safely. In four days, everything had changed.

Since Aunt Sara needed the car the next day, Stacy and her cousins took the bus to school. Although they preferred the faster, smoother ride of the car, the bus wasn't that bad. It stopped at all the farms between Summerdale and Douglasville, so they had a chance to visit with their friends on the way to school.

Since Tricia always called if she had the use of a car, Stacy knew before the bus stopped that Tricia was going to be on the bus, too. Hal and Chris claimed seats near the front, but Stacy and Angie went toward the back and joined Tricia and her little sister.

Tricia looked about as happy as Stacy felt, but she managed a smile for her friend. "Did your mother and Joni get off all right yesterday?" she asked.

Stacy nodded. "What about Chuck?"

"He left late yesterday afternoon. I know he has to go back to college, but it gets harder every time he leaves."

"How do you stand it?" Stacy asked.

"Well, I give myself permission to feel rotten—to wallow in self-pity for a full twenty-four hours. Then I dry my eyes and get on with whatever I have to do."

"And that works?" Stacy asked.

"I make it. Every time I start to think about how much I miss Chuck, I remind myself that I've already cried about it. I make myself think about something else," Tricia said. "If you'll just bear with me and help me make it to four o'clock this afternoon, I'll be all right again."

So much for unloading my problems on her, Stacy thought. But one day wasn't too much to give her friend. Besides, maybe things between Lane and her would improve if she just gave it a little time.

"Will it help if I remind you that Christmas is only a month away?" Stacy asked. "Chuck will be home for a couple of weeks then."

"That will make me feel better tomorrow," Tricia said. "Today, nothing's going to help."

The bus made its next stop at the Broussards'. Yvette Broussard took the seat behind Hal and Chris, but Andrea joined Tricia and Stacy.

"I see I'm not the only one who's been reduced to riding the bus," she said. "Isn't this the pits? My birthday's so close to Christmas, I've been trying to convince my parents to combine all of my gifts into one big present—like maybe a car."

"That's nice," Tricia murmured.

"Drew told me about his date Friday night," Andrea continued. "If I didn't think he was trying to make me jealous, I might believe that he was really impressed with that girl from Pennsylvania."

"They seemed to have a good time," Stacy said.

"I'm glad they did," Andrea said. "I've dated Drew a few times, and you know how Douglasville is. If I'm not careful, everyone will think we're dating each other exclusively. I don't want that to happen now."

When Andrea turned around, Tricia whispered to Stacy, "She's probably thinking about the Christmas dance."

"What do you mean?" Stacy asked.

Tricia shrugged. "You probably shouldn't pay any attention to me. I'm in such a lousy mood, I'm suspecting the worst of everyone today."

"Okay, you've warned me. Now tell me what you're talking about."

"The Key Club sponsors a big dance right before Christmas every year. That's when they present the new court and announce their Sweetheart for the coming year."

"I still don't understand," Stacy said.

"The boys nominate five junior girls to be on the court, and they get to serve as hostesses for the club and help with the fund raisers and whatever. Of course, only one of the girls can be the Sweetheart."

"And you think Andrea—"

Tricia didn't wait for her to finish the sentence. "Uh-huh. I figure she's going to be campaigning like mad for the next two weeks, and it's a little hard to flirt with the entire Key Club when you have a boyfriend hanging around you."

"Do you think she has a chance?"

"I'm almost positive she'll be on the court, but she's got some stiff competition for Sweetheart. Only the boys in the club get to vote, and if they vote for personality, it could go to Theresa Averett. But then, Regina Dawson has one brother in the Key Club and another one who'll be in it next year. They could swing the vote for her. Of course, if you go on looks alone, Andrea probably has the best chance."

Stacy couldn't resist teasing Tricia. "How did you get to be Sweetheart?"

"Last year almost every boy in the Key Club had a girlfriend. I figured all of them who didn't have a girlfriend on the court must have voted for me just to keep their girlfriends from getting jealous."

"And you're so modest, too," Stacy said.

Tricia grinned, "Yes, aren't I, though?"

When the bus finally stopped at school, Stacy and Tricia waited until the younger kids had pushed and shoved their way off the bus before gathering up their own books. Since they were both seniors in the college preparatory program, they had practically the same schedule.

The only exception was fourth period. Since Stacy had already completed two years of French at Brantwood, she took home economics fourth period when Tricia took Spanish. They met in the cafeteria for lunch immediately afterward.

"I know why I'm so miserable," Tricia said, setting her tray on an empty table, "but what's your problem? Are you beginning to regret transferring to Douglasville High instead of going to that fancy boarding school with Joni?"

"Good heavens, no," Stacy said. "But that's all right. I don't want to unload on you. My problems will wait until tomorrow."

"No, go ahead, tell me. It'll give me something else to think about."

"It's just . . . Tricia, have I changed that much?"

Tricia thought for a minute. "No, not really. Of course, you've learned a lot more about the people here and what it's like to live on a farm, but I'd say you're pretty much the same person you were when I first met you. Why?"

"Joni said I've changed. I think she found me boring."

"And that bothers you?"

Stacy shook her head. "I can deal with that. But with all the attention Lane was paying Joni, compared to her, maybe he thinks I'm boring, too."

"You don't really believe that."

"Well, you saw him at Drury's. He paid more attention to her than he did to me," Stacy said. She attacked her mashed potatoes, poking holes in them with her fork, but made no attempt to eat them. "Do you know that the first time I met Lane, Aunt Sara sent him to pick me up at the bus stop in Summerdale. I got off the bus, and he said, 'I'm Lane. There's the truck, get in.' When he and Joni met, she kissed him on the cheek and he told her she was pretty."

"Maybe he was just trying to make you jealous."

"Lane's not like that and you know it."

"Have you talked to him?"

"I tried to talk to him Saturday night, but he wouldn't. Mom and Joni were still here so I didn't want to make a scene, but he hasn't called or come by since they left."

"What about Friday night? You'll have your usual date with him, won't you?"

"I don't know. Right now, I don't know anything."

"Well, I do," Tricia said. "I know how Lane feels about you, and believe me, it's all going to work out."

The bell rang, and the girls picked up their trays. "Can I get that in writing?" Stacy asked as they made their way to their lockers.

With things the way they were between her and Lane, Stacy didn't know whether she should go to the dairy that afternoon and run the risk of seeing him or wait and let him seek her out. Before she could make up her mind about what to do, Aunt Sara took the decision out of her hands by asking her to run an errand in Douglasville.

Tuesday, Stacy had to stay after school to work on a research paper for her English class, and when she hadn't seen or heard anything from Lane by Wednesday afternoon, she knew he was purposely avoiding her.

Normally, if he didn't see her sometime during the day, he would call her before she went to bed that night. Sometimes, he'd do both. He had never gone four days without seeing her, even if he had to invent an excuse to come to her aunt's.

She knew enough about his schedule that she could have arranged to see him, but since she wasn't sure it was the right thing to do, she did nothing. Finally, when she got home from school Friday afternoon, Aunt Sara had a message from Lane.

"Lane had to go to the stockyards, but he said to tell you he'd be here at seven-thirty. He said if you wanted to do something else, just call Kate and leave word with her."

Stacy knew Lane was giving her a way out, but she had no intention of taking it. "Seven-thirty's fine," she said.

"Are y'all going to the basketball game?" Hal asked.

"They're playing in Demopolis tonight, so I doubt it," Stacy said. "I'll take you back to the school to catch the pep squad bus if you want to go."

"That's okay, I'll catch a ride with somebody else."

Stacy could have used a pep talk from Tricia, but she knew her friend would be getting ready for the game. She had to face this alone.

She could deal with her jealousy over the attention Lane had paid Joni, and the fact that he hadn't called or come to see her all week. What really hurt was that he didn't care whether or not she left Summerdale.

She would never forget how alone and unwanted she had felt when her parents first sent her to Summerdale. It had been Lane who, having lost his own parents, best understood her sense of abandonment. His love had helped her get past all that, or at least she thought she had. Now all of her old fears were coming back. When it suited their purpose, her parents didn't really care where she lived, and obviously neither did Lane.

Stacy tried to stay busy all afternoon so she wouldn't have to think about what might happen that night. She helped Chris feed the calves, went horseback riding with Angie and still had time to bathe and dress before Lane arrived.

She was so nervous she actually jumped when she heard Smokey's bark. You'd think this was my first date with him, she thought, and then smiled. By the time she and Lane got around to going on a real date, she hadn't been nervous at all. This was different. Maybe it was because she was afraid it was going to be their last date.

When she walked into the kitchen, Lane was talking to Uncle Jim and Aunt Sara.

"Where are you two going tonight?" Aunt Sara asked.

Lane glanced at Stacy, and when she shrugged, he said, "I guess we'll see the movie in Douglasville. We won't be late."

"Just be careful," Uncle Jim said from where he sat on the sofa.

With the awful tension between them, the ten miles into Douglasville seemed more like twenty. Even the movie didn't help. Five seconds after it started, Stacy couldn't remember its name or who was in it. She was, however, keenly aware that Lane didn't reach for her hand. Once, he stretched and put his arm around the back of her seat, but he was careful not to touch her.

They sat like two statues, staring at the screen until the movie was over.

"Would you like to stop by the Dairy Queen before we go home?" Lane asked on their way out of the theater.

Stacy's mouth was so dry she didn't try to speak and just shook her head.

They were almost home before Lane spoke again. "You're awfully quiet tonight."

Suddenly something inside Stacy snapped. If this was going to be their last date, it wasn't going to end this way. "Maybe I just seem quiet because Joni's not around," she said.

"What's that supposed to mean?"

"You were a lot friendlier when she was here."

"I thought that was the idea. Didn't you want me to be nice to your friend?"

"That didn't include kissing her!"

"I didn't kiss her—she kissed me."

"I didn't know there was a difference."

"Well, believe me, there is," Lane ground out. He pulled into the Colbys' driveway and stopped the car. "But we both know that isn't what this is all about."

Now it was Stacy's turn to ask "What do you mean?"

"I think Joni and your mother got you to wondering if you made a mistake about coming back here to live. You probably figure that if we break up, you won't have any reason to stay."

"What do you care? You told Mother it was all right with you!"

"I didn't say it like that."

"But that's what you meant. You never wanted me here in the first place. You've just been waiting for me to admit I was wrong."

"Can you honestly say that you haven't had any doubts?" Lane asked.

The anger drained out of Stacy, leaving her weak and shaken. "No," she said softly. "I guess I can't."

Since it was obvious that one of them was going to have to say it, Stacy wanted to be the one. "Maybe we should both take a step backward and think about... things."

"Maybe we should," he said.

Tears were already beginning to well up in Stacy's eyes, so she felt for the door handle and slipped out of the car before Lane could move.

She hurried into the house without looking back.

Chapter Six

Sleepless nights were getting to be the rule for Stacy, so she wasn't surprised that this one was no exception. At two, she heard Smokey chasing a squirrel through the yard, and at four, Uncle Jim got up. She heard him moving around in his room and then tap on the boys' door as he started up the hall.

Obviously he and Hal were milking this morning. That meant Lane had the morning off, she thought before she caught herself. She had to stop thinking of everything as it related to Lane. What they had was over—finished.

She waited until the truck left and then, unable to stand the confines of the bed any longer, she slipped out from under the leg Angie had thrown over her and headed for the kitchen and a cup of coffee.

Her aunt was there ahead of her.

"I didn't hear you get up," Stacy said in greeting.

"You were in the bathroom when I came up the hall," Aunt Sara said. Noticing Stacy's face and the red-ringed eyes, she asked, "Are you all right?"

Stacy knew that she wouldn't be able to keep it a secret. "Lane and I broke up last night."

"I'm so sorry. Is there anything I can do for...either of you?"

Stacy shook her head. "No, but don't worry. We didn't have a big argument or anything. You won't have to choose sides between us."

"Well, I admit I'm glad about that. You're both very special to me."

Stacy brought her coffee to the table and sat down beside her aunt. "Did you ever regret your decision to marry Uncle Jim instead of going away to college the way Mom did?"

"Frequently," Aunt Sara said, and then smiled at the expression on Stacy's face. "Don't get me wrong, Jim was never the problem. I just wish that we had waited until I went to college or a vocational school for some kind of training."

"Really?"

"Well, you know how things are on a farm. We seem to be caught in either feast or famine. A lot of farmers, right here in Douglasville, have lost their homes. When money gets tight, I wish there was something I could do to help. And I can't help worrying about what would happen if Jim was in an accident and couldn't work. I don't want Hal to have to step in and take his place."

"You mean the way Lane did when his parents died?"

Aunt Sara nodded. "Of course, Lane's a fine young man, so I can't say that it's hurt him, but he did lose part of his childhood. I don't want that for Hal or Chris."

"I hadn't thought about that," Stacy said.

With the first light of day, the calves in the pen outside began bawling for their breakfast. Stacy and her aunt took care of them together. Afterward, Aunt Sara made up a short grocery order for Stacy to fill in Douglasville.

On her way home, she stopped by the Allens' to see Tricia.

"Since Chuck is away at school, I thought you might want to get together tonight. I could use the company," Stacy said.

"Oh, no, what happened?" Tricia asked.

"Lane and I broke up last night."

"Why? Tell me what happened."

"I'm not really sure. We were talking about...well, I guess we were arguing about Joni, and then he told me I was just using her as an excuse to break up with him. He thinks I want to move back East with Mom or Dad."

"Did you tell him that wasn't true?"

"No," Stacy said firmly. "Don't you see? If he really believed that, then why wasn't he trying to convince me to stay?"

"Maybe he thought he shouldn't have to," Tricia said.

"Or maybe I've been fooling myself all along," Stacy said. She took a deep breath. "Tricia, what am I going to do?"

"Spend the night with me, we'll talk, and cry, and stick pins in pictures of Lane. I guarantee you'll feel better tomorrow morning."

"Thanks, I don't know what I'd do without you. I really need a friend tonight."

"You've got one," Tricia said.

On Monday, Tricia gave Stacy a ride to school. When they arrived, a group of girls were waiting for them in the parking lot.

"Is it true?" someone asked before Stacy got out of the car. "Did you and Lane really break up? What happened?"

Stacy was too shocked to say anything, and she automatically turned to Tricia for help.

"They just decided to see other people," Tricia said.

The girls were staring at Stacy with such open concern, Stacy felt she had to say something. "It's all right, really. We just decided to cool it for a while. It's not as though we're mortal enemies or anything. We're still part of the same family."

"When I heard Yvette Broussard say that Andrea had a date with Lane on Saturday night, I didn't believe her," one girl said as she walked away. "I guess I owe her an apology."

Stacy's body stiffened, and Tricia had to nudge her to get her moving again.

Once they were away from the other girls, Stacy exploded, "Can you believe it? Friday night he tells me that I'm the one who wants to break up, and Saturday he has a date with Andrea Broussard! That can't be just a coincidence!"

Tricia pinched Stacy's arm, hard. "Pretend you're talking about our homework or the weather," she ordered tersely.

"Wha—"

Tricia's expression was totally blank. She even managed to smile and wave at someone walking past them while she said, "Everyone's going to be watching you today. Unless you want Lane and Andrea to know exactly how upset you were when you found out about them, you'd better act as though nothing's happened."

"How am I supposed to do that?"

"You just do, that's all," Tricia said. "Now smile, and let's get to class."

Charlotte Townsend, a girl from their history class, joined them at their lockers. "I just heard," she told Stacy. "Why on earth did you break up with Lane?"

Stacy managed a little shrug. "We just agreed to see other people."

"Oh gosh, I don't know who else you'd want to see around here. Lane is so handsome."

"I know. It's nothing against him, but after this year we'll be going our separate ways. . . ." She let her voice trail off and changed the subject. "Providing, I graduate, of course. We didn't have any history homework over Thanksgiving, did we?"

Stacy glanced over at Tricia as Charlotte started flipping through her notebook, and Tricia signaled her approval.

Stacy sighed. Maybe she could do it.

Having made it over the first hurdle, she thought she was ready to face the rest of the day, but it was impossible to anticipate who was going to bring up the subject of Lane or what kind of personal questions they would ask.

The entire day was one long obstacle course. By three o'clock, Stacy was convinced that everyone in the county knew that she and Lane had broken up.

She was on her way to the car with Tricia when Hal caught up with her. "I have to stay and help put out the collection boxes that we're using to collect Christmas toys for needy children," he said. "I'll get a ride home with Yvette."

"I'll tell Aunt Sara where you are," Stacy said. "You want me to take your books for you?"

"Thanks." He handed them over to her. "By the way, have you heard the rumors about Lane that have been going around today?"

"They're true, Hal," Stacy said. "We aren't dating anymore."

"I know all about that," he said. "Mama told us about it so that Angie wouldn't ask you a lot of dumb questions."

"What rumors are you talking about?" Tricia asked.

"The stuff about Lane having a date with Andrea Saturday night," he said.

"You mean he didn't?" Stacy asked.

"I know he didn't. Lane and I went to Mississippi to pick up a horse Mr. Broussard's giving Yvette for Christmas—by the way, that's a secret. After we got back, we stopped by their house to let Mr. Broussard know we had the horse in the stables at Grandma's, and Andrea was there. She hung around, and we talked to her for a while and then went home. If that was a date, she had it with both of us."

"But Yvette's been saying..."

"Do you want me to go around and straighten everyone out?" Hal asked.

Before Stacy could reply, Tricia said, "That's okay, Hal. Just let it drop."

"But it's not true," Stacy said.

"I know, but why stir up more gossip over something that's not even important?" Tricia asked.

Hal was waiting for her answer, and Stacy didn't want him to feel as though he were caught in the middle. After all, he was Lane's cousin, too.

"I guess Tricia's right," she said. "Lane and I broke up Friday night, so it really wouldn't have mattered if he had had a date with Andrea on Saturday."

"That's what I thought," Hal said, "but I figured I'd check with you anyway."

After Hal left, Stacy fumed. "I don't see why you wouldn't let him tell everyone the truth."

"Because Andrea and Yvette have probably done you a favor," Tricia said. "If the boys around here think that Lane has started dating other girls, they'll know you're fair game."

"What a romantic way of putting it," Stacy said dryly. "Not that it matters. I'm not interested in dating anymore."

"Well, you can't sit at home all the time," Tricia said. "You don't have to think of it as replacing Lane. Just go out with boys you like as friends. You know, whether you're moping at home or out with friends—you're still going to have to live through the same number of hours. Besides," she added after a minute's hesitation, "the Key Club's Christmas dance is coming up. You have to go to that."

"Why? I'm not in the court, and if Andrea Broussard is going to be the new Sweetheart—well, I think I can stand to miss that. Especially if she's going to be escorted by Lane Colby."

"That's exactly why you have to go," Tricia said.

"I don't understand."

"If Lane takes a date to that dance and you don't even show up, people are going to remember it. You can grow up, get married and move away, but every time you come back, they'll wonder if you ever got over that crush you had on Lane."

"You don't mean that," Stacy said.

"You've been living here for six months. You've seen how the people are," Tricia said. "You're always saying how lucky we are to live in a place where everyone cares about everyone else. That may be true, but because they care, they also take a greater than average interest in your personal life. It's a trade off—you have to take the bad with the good."

"What if no one asks me to the dance?"

"Don't worry, we'll come up with something," Tricia assured her.

"I'm not so sure," Stacy said. She groped in her purse for her car keys. "Let's go. What do you bet, Angie's waiting for me by the door with something she just has to tell me right away?"

Sure enough, Angie popped out of the house as soon as she heard the car pull up. She was waving a piece of paper.

"Two boys called you, Stacy! Mama said they might want to ask you for a date! Are you going to be dating a lot of boys now that you don't love Lane anymore?"

Stacy's face flamed.

Aunt Sara had followed Angie out the door. "That's enough, Angie," she said. She shook her head. "Sometimes I think you have a lot of your grandmother in you."

"No, I don't. She's old."

"Just give Stacy her messages and go...count out the bottles so we can feed the calves."

Angie handed Stacy the paper. "That's not all," she said. "Mama, tell her about the other one."

"Angie, go!" her mother ordered.

Stacy looked back at her aunt. "I had another call?" she asked.

Aunt Sara looked uncomfortable. "I was going to tell you about it, but...well, Lane was here. He was here to get Chris to help at the dairy, and he answered the telephone."

"Who was it?" Stacy asked.

"I don't know. He said it was for you and then walked out. Were you expecting a call from someone?"

"No, not really," Stacy said. She looked down at the names on the paper Angie had given her. Bobby Hall and Drew Riley. "Did they say what they wanted?"

"No, I just assumed they were calling you about a date. I'm sorry about Angie. I guess I'll have to be more careful about what I say in front of her."

"It's all right. After the day I've had, Angie's the least of my problems," Stacy said, tucking the telephone numbers in one of her books. "By the way, Hal asked me to tell you that he had to stay after school. I'll go help Angie take care of the calves."

Although Hal and Chris could almost handle the calves by themselves by the time they were six, Angie's help consisted of telling others how it was supposed to be done. Uncle Jim insisted that Angie's habit of sticking her pert little nose in everything meant she was going to be a good manager. Her grandmother said it just meant that she was nosy.

Stacy didn't really mind. She enjoyed helping spoil her youngest cousin. Still, she was glad that Hal got home in time to help her finish cleaning up. They were walking back to the house when Lane drove up with Chris.

Stacy was torn between hoping that he would simply drop Chris off and leave, and wanting him to stay. When he turned the engine off and got out of the truck, her heart lurched madly.

She tried to pretend that his presence didn't affect her, but she didn't have to worry. Chris was so excited he commanded everyone's attention.

"Guess what? We're invited to go on a deer hunt. It's going to be this Saturday!"

Hal looked at Lane. "Are we going? Dad's not going to make us miss it, is he?"

"That's what I'm here to find out," Lane said.

Before coming to Alabama, Stacy had seen deer only in zoos. But she had learned to look for the shy, graceful animals at the edge of the woods and fields. Once she and Chris had watched a doe with twin fawns at the creek.

"Why are you hunting deer?" she asked.

"To eat," Chris said. "Haven't you ever eaten venison?"

"I don't think so," she said.

"It's good. You'll like it," Hal said.

Stacy stared at her cousins. She couldn't believe what they were saying. "But there are plenty of other good things to eat, you don't have to kill... Bambi!"

Turning her back on them, she stalked off toward the house. Her cousins, significantly subdued, followed her.

Behind them, Lane's eyes glowed with amusement. He couldn't help it. She really was something when she was all fired up.

The boys forgot their embarrassment as soon as they saw their father. They both started in at once to ask him about the hunt.

"I've already heard about it," Jim Colby said. "Charles Broussard saw me this morning."

"Are we going?" Hal asked.

"I guess we can take the day off," Jim said. "What do you think, Lane?"

Lane nodded. "That's what I told him."

"Can I go with y'all this year?" Chris asked. "You promised!"

"You can come with me," his father said. "I figure you and I'll handle the morning milking and let Lane and Hal go out with the first group of hunters."

"Then we'll come home at noon and take over the afternoon milking," Lane said.

"What about me?" Angie asked. "I want to go, too."

"Oh, Angie, not you, too!" Stacy exclaimed.

In the silence that followed, Lane said, "Stacy doesn't think much of deer hunting."

"It may sound cruel, but hunting is the best way to manage the deer herds. Deer don't have any natural predators around here, and if hunters didn't periodically thin out the herds, eventually, there would be just too many of them," her uncle said. "They would either start eating our crops or starve to death. And we don't shoot any does or fawns. This hunt is just for bucks."

Her uncle's argument made sense to Stacy, but she didn't want to listen to them discussing the hunt. She hadn't taken off her jacket, so when they began talking about the guns and ammunition they would need, she slipped back outside.

She was still sitting in the swing when Lane came back out.

At first she thought he was going to walk past her without speaking, but at the last minute, he stopped.

"You can go back inside now. I'm leaving," he said.

"That's not why I'm out here."

"Then why are you? Are you waiting for a date?"

Looking for a way to wipe the smug look off his face, Stacy said, "Aunt Sara said you took a phone call for me this afternoon. Would you mind telling me who it was?"

Lane shrugged. "I don't know."

"Then why didn't you write it down? If you're going to take messages..."

"Stacy, he hung up without leaving his name," Lane said. "I wouldn't worry about it, though. If he doesn't call back, I'm sure someone else will."

Stacy jumped up from the swing. Her face was burning. "As a matter of fact, they already have," she said. She paused before heading for the door. "Several, in fact!" she added.

Chapter Seven

As angry as she was at Lane, Stacy still put off returning her telephone calls until after dinner. If Bobby and Drew were calling her for a date, she wanted to give them every chance to give up and call someone else.

When she couldn't wait any longer, she took the paper with their numbers on it into her aunt's bedroom and closed the door for privacy. She knew Drew better than Bobby, so she called him first. After stumbling over her own name, she finally managed to say "Aunt Sara said you called."

"Rumor has it that you and Lane Colby broke up," Drew said. "If you don't already have a date to the basketball tournament on Saturday night, I'd like to take you."

He said it so casually, so matter-of-factly, Stacy's embarrassment fled. "Thanks, I'd like to go," she said.

"There's going to be four teams in the play-offs that night, so we should probably get there early," Drew said. "What if I pick you up around six-thirty?"

"That sounds fine, and who knows, maybe Douglasville will win this one."

He chuckled. "Now, that would be something, wouldn't it?" he said. "Good night, I'll see you in school tomorrow."

Stacy hung up the telephone, and then before she lost her nerve, she dialed Bobby Hall's number. Bobby lived about halfway between Summerdale and Douglasville, and even though he was in one of her classes, she didn't feel quite as comfortable with him.

She let him lead the conversation, and after chatting about their homework, their teacher, and even their textbook, he finally got around to talking about Lane. Eventually he asked her out.

Stacy kept her refusal very general. "I'm sorry, but I've already made plans for this weekend. Maybe another time."

Before he could suggest anything specific, she added, "I have to go now. Uncle Jim wants to use the telephone."

She replaced the receiver with a sigh. She had accepted a date with one boy and refused one with another. That was what average high school girls did. They had lots of friends, dated a wide variety of boys, and had lots of fun. She hated it. Her date with Drew was the first she'd had in five months except Lane. Was Lane dating, too? Would he bring her to the game? She felt sad thinking about it.

She was, however, glad to have something to report to Tricia the next morning. "I decided to go ahead and get it over with. I have a date with Drew Riley for the basketball tournament in Douglasville Saturday night."

"And I can see that you're really throwing yourself into the spirit of it, too," Tricia said dryly.

"I'm sorry, I didn't mean for it to sound that way. I like Drew. I really do. It's just that—"

"You're doing the right thing," Tricia said, interrupting Stacy before she could bring up Lane's name. "When Chuck first went back to college this fall, I was absolutely miserable. But I reminded myself—this is my senior year. I made up my mind to enjoy all the ball games, the club functions and the parties. It doesn't change the way I feel about Chuck."

"I am going to try to have a good time at the game."

"And at the Key Club's Christmas dance."

"Wait a minute," Stacy said. "I'm not that fast. I'm going to have to work up to dances gradually."

"That's all right," Tricia said. "I've got it all figured out. Chuck has this really nice roommate at college, and I thought..."

"You don't mean a blind date?" Stacy asked.

"Why not? He's nice. I haven't actually met him, but I've talked to him on the telephone."

Stacy hesitated. "I don't know, Tricia."

"Chuck's calling me Friday night. Why don't you come over and spend the night with me? Then when Chuck calls, you can talk to his roommate."

"I'll come over, but I can't spend the night. I have to take care of the calves Saturday morning."

"Well, plan to stay as late as you can," Tricia said. "We'll play everything else by ear."

"I'll do that. I did tell Bobby Hall that I had plans, and besides, it beats staying at home wondering what Lane's doing."

Her aunt and uncle didn't like Stacy to drive alone at night, but Tricia Allen lived only a few miles away. Still, Stacy had to call home when she arrived at Tricia's and promise to call again when she started home.

Chuck called precisely at eight. After he and Tricia talked for a while, Stacy talked to his roommate, Ken Bilderback. Actually Ken did most of the talking. Stacy felt awkward trying to flirt, or even be friendly, with a stranger. Only after Tricia whispered a remark about Lane did Stacy finally agree to go with Ken to the Christmas dance.

She didn't want to think about Lane or where he might be tonight.

Since he didn't have any reason to hurry home, Lane took his time cleaning up the dairy after he finished the evening milking. After dinner, he did some bookwork, entering information about the cows into their permanent records from the notebook he kept at the barn.

If his grandmother thought it was strange for him to stay home on a Friday night, she didn't say anything, and for his grandmother, that was unusual itself. She wasn't known for keeping her opinions to herself. Last summer she had been the only one to warn him about what would happen if he let himself get close to Stacy. "Stacy's a nice girl who's going to be leaving soon," she had told him.

If he had taken her advice, he would have missed the past few months with Stacy, but he wouldn't be sitting here with his stomach in a knot.

When he couldn't stand it any longer, he walked outside. Without any particular destination in mind, he walked to the edge of the grove of trees and stared out toward Jim's house. Everything there was quiet, too. The only light he could see was the one outside the back door—the one Jim and Sara left on whenever Stacy was out.

He wasn't surprised. Boys had lined up for dates with her before he started dating her. Around eleven, a car turned into Jim's driveway, and a minute or so later, the light over the back door went out. At last he could relax. She was home.

Stacy got up early the next morning. With Chris at the dairy with his father and Hal getting ready to go hunting, she had to take care of the calves. She was almost in the kitchen before she heard Aunt Sara talking and realized that Lane was in there, too.

It was too late to worry about her lack of makeup and the fact that her hair was a mass of unruly curls. She lifted her chin and forged ahead.

"Good morning, Aunt Sara. I'll go ahead and take care of the calves and have my breakfast later."

"You've got time for a cup of coffee first," her aunt said. "The calves aren't even up yet."

"No, that's all right."

"She's still angry about the hunt," Hal said. "She hasn't even spoken to me this morning."

"I'll talk to you all day—if you'll stay home," Stacy said.

"Aw, Stacy, don't be that way," he protested. "I'm almost fifteen years old, and I've never even shot at a deer before. Lane was only twelve when he got that set of antlers over Grandma's fireplace."

Stacy had avoided looking directly at Lane, but now she couldn't help it. "You shot that deer?" she asked him.

She had no right to look so fresh and pretty, Lane thought irrationally. Not after the night that he'd spent. "No, Stacy," he said dryly, "he just walked into the yard and donated his antlers."

Stung by his sarcasm, Stacy picked up her coat and started out of the door ahead of him.

"The idea of displaying part of an animal's body as some kind of trophy is barbaric," she said coolly.

She was headed for the milk shed, but she saw Lane pause beside the pickup and hand Hal a bright orange vest. Watching Hal pull it on over his jacket, she couldn't resist one last jab.

"At least you're giving the deer a fair chance. With that vest on, they should be able to see you coming."

"Deer are color blind, Stacy," Hal said.

"The vest is so that the other hunters will see him," Lane added.

Stacy looked back at Hal. In her concern for the animals, she hadn't even considered that the woods would be full of men with guns. "Hal, you will be careful, won't you?"

"Oh, sure," he said.

Hal had started around to the passenger's side while Lane reached for the door on the driver's side. Momentarily distracted by the pull of the material across his broad shoulders, Stacy suddenly realized that Lane wasn't wearing one of the safety vests.

"Don't you have one of those orange things?" she asked him.

"I'll put it on when I get there," he said offhandedly, and then because her concern sounded so genuine, he grinned. "I didn't know you cared."

"Of course I do. I'd hate to see any dumb animal get shot!" she snapped before turning her back on him.

Working quickly, she fed the calves and hurried back to the warmth of the house. She poured herself a cup of coffee and cradled the cup in her hands.

"Has it started to warm up outside?" her aunt asked.

"Let me put it this way," Stacy said. "If I could figure out how to do it, I'd climb inside this cup."

"I hope Hal and Chris put on enough clothes. It can get so cold on those deer stands."

"How can you stand it?" Stacy asked. "Knowing they're out there with all those guns."

"It's not easy. I generally try to stay as busy as possible. Today I thought I might start my Christmas baking."

Angie appeared in the doorway as if by magic. "Can I help?" she asked. "And Stacy, too?"

"If she wants to," Aunt Sara said, taking out her recipe file and bringing it to the table. "While you two have your breakfast, we'll decide what kind of cookies we want to make."

"Chocolate chip," Angie said.

"Brownies," Stacy added.

"And I think I'll bake a fruit cake today," Sara said.

Angie made a face. "Yuk."

"I know," her mother said, "but it wouldn't be Christmas without at least one fruit cake. Between now and New Year's Eve, someone will eat it."

"With Hal and Chris around how on earth do you manage to keep any cookies until Christmas?" Stacy asked.

"I leave a few out and hide the rest in the freezer," Aunt Sara said.

Within a few hours, the house was full of the delicious aroma of melting chocolate and warm spices. "I don't remember our house ever smelling like this," Stacy said. "I think Mother ordered all of our Christmas cookies from a bakery."

"Did you leave cookies out for Santa?" Angie asked.

"Sure, I put them right underneath the tree."

"Why didn't you leave them beside the fireplace like I do?" Angie asked.

"We didn't have a fireplace."

"Then how did Santa get into your house?"

"I don't know, but he managed it somehow. I always had presents on Christmas morning," Stacy said.

Angie looked at her mother closely. "Maybe that's because Santa Claus is really just your mama and daddy."

Aunt Sara shrugged. "All I can tell you is that he won't come at all if you don't believe in him."

"Oh, I believe," Angie said. "And I know exactly what I want him to bring me."

Angie repeated her list of wants, making additions and deletions as they occurred to her, while they worked through the morning. At noon, they stopped for a sandwich and a cup of soup, and afterward, Aunt Sara sent Angie to her room to write a letter to

Santa while she and Stacy began cleaning up the kitchen.

Stacy had forgotten all about the time until she turned from putting away the last mixing bowl and caught Aunt Sara staring out of the window. She realized that her aunt had been glancing toward the window for some time.

"What time did Lane say he and Hal would be back?" she asked.

"Around noon. Neither one of them took a lunch."

"You don't think—" Stacy started, but her aunt cut her off.

"No, I don't. This wouldn't be the first time they got busy and forgot about eating."

Stacy wanted to believe her, but every passing minute made it harder to stay away from the window. The Colby men might forget about lunch, but they wouldn't forget about milking. And it was getting closer and closer to start-up time.

Finally a truck stopped in front of the house. Stacy and her aunt watched, holding their breaths, until Hal got out. When the truck drove off, they hurried to meet him at the door.

"Have y'all heard from Lane?" Hal asked when he saw them.

"He was supposed to be with you," his mother said.

"I came out of the woods a couple of hours ago. I waited at our truck, and when he didn't show up, I got a ride home with Chuck Hastings's father."

"You just left him?" Stacy asked.

"He still has the truck," Hal said, "but I knew somebody had to get home and start milking. Mama, can you make me a couple of sandwiches? And Stacy, I'll need you to help me at the barn."

"What are we going to do about Lane? We can't just forget him," Stacy said.

"We're not going to do that," Aunt Sara said. "You and Hal go on to the dairy, and I'll see what I can find out. Try not to worry. I'll call Kate and see if she's heard anything."

Stacy was glad to have something to do to keep her busy, but the sick feeling in her stomach wouldn't go away. What if something had happened to Lane? What if he were hurt? Right this minute, he could be lying in the woods, bleeding.

She and Hal washed down the barn and all the milking equipment with disinfectant before they let the first group of cows inside. They had already started milking when they heard the distinctive sound of a pickup truck.

Without a word, they rushed to the door and saw Lane climb out of his truck and start toward them.

A wave of relief washed over Stacy, leaving her so weak that she had to lean against the side of the barn. He was all right. He wasn't limping, and as far as she could see, there wasn't even a bandage.

Lane smiled, and suddenly Stacy saw red. All that worrying for nothing!

"Where on earth have you been?" she asked.

"I was hunting, and I—"

"You were supposed to be back hours ago! You know what time we have to start milking."

Hal was standing behind Stacy, and he interrupted her tirade to ask quietly, "What happened?"

"Gary Broussard got hurt."

"Gary? I didn't even see him this morning," Hal said. "Was he shot?"

"No, he wasn't even hunting. He was in the back of their land cutting up some dead trees for firewood, and his chain saw slipped. He cut his foot."

"How bad was it?" Hal asked.

"It wasn't good," Lane said. "The saw cut all the way through his boot. The way the blood was bubbling up through it, I couldn't tell if it took off part of the foot or not. I didn't take the time to check it out. I just got him to the hospital."

The color that had flooded Stacy's face suddenly evaporated, leaving her as white as a sheet.

"Are you all right?" Lane asked.

Stacy couldn't speak, but she managed to nod. Without a word, Lane held out his arms, and she walked into them without hesitation.

"How did you happen to find him?" Hal asked.

"I was following a deer that had been shot. I didn't know if it was just hurt or if I needed to finish him off. Luckily Gary heard my shot. If he hadn't, I don't think..."

Stacy shivered. Gary wasn't even hunting. It was an accident that could happen to anyone, anytime.

"Why don't you go on home," Lane suggested. "Hal and I can finish the milking."

He started to walk her back to the truck, and she remembered something. "Did you shoot the deer?"

"It was hurt. I had to put it out of its misery."

"I'm sure it appreciated your concern," she said, twisting out of his grasp. "You know, you could have shown some concern for...Sara and Hal. They were worried about you!"

"I was in the woods, Stacy. There weren't any telephones. After I got Gary to the hospital, I called the

Broussards first, and then as soon as I could, I called Grandma."

Stacy was already in the truck, and she started the engine before he was finished, so he didn't know if she heard him or not. With a muttered curse, he turned back to the barn.

It was just as well, he reminded himself.

When Stacy got home, Sara had a basket of their freshly baked cookies ready to go. "Take these over to the Broussards and find out if there's anything we can do," she said.

Stacy left immediately, and when she rang the Broussards doorbell, Andrea and Yvette answered it together. They looked so pale and shaken that Stacy was almost ashamed that she had been so selfishly relieved that it hadn't been Lane or Hal who had been injured.

"Have you heard anything from the hospital?" Stacy asked.

Andrea shook her head. "Not since they transferred Gary to Sheffield. Dr. McAdory stopped the bleeding and sent him directly to a specialist. They're operating on him right now... reattaching his foot. Mom said she'd call as soon as the operation was over."

"Aunt Sara sent me to ask if there was anything we could do," Stacy said.

"I don't think so. My brother Dan has already called Drew to help out at the dairy until Gary's... back," Andrea said.

"What about the cooking and housework?"

"That's all taken care of, too. Mrs. Kate called and told me not to do anything. She said she would arrange for someone to take care of that. And Dan's wife, Sallie, is coming over to stay with us while Dan goes to the hospital to be with Mom and Dad."

The telephone rang, and Andrea broke off to wait for Yvette to answer it. Yvette shook her head. It wasn't the hospital.

"I'll tell Aunt Sara you're all right," Stacy said, "but please don't hesitate to call us if you need anything."

"Well, I just remembered the basketball game," Andrea said. "I don't want to tie up the telephone in case Mom tries to call, but I am a cheerleader. I should let someone know that I won't be at the game tonight."

"I'll call Tricia for you as soon as I get home," Stacy said.

Before she went home, she made one more stop at the Broussards' barn. She waited at the door for Drew to notice her.

"Anything wrong?" he asked.

"I just got through talking to Andrea. She said you were helping out here, so I thought I'd tell you that if you wanted to skip the game tonight, I'll understand."

"I'm going to be late," Drew said. "Dan wants to get out of here and get over to the hospital as soon as he can, so I'll have to stay and clean up."

"It's all right."

"Why don't we meet at the game?" Drew asked. "Do you think you could get a ride to the school?"

"I'll ask Tricia. I need to call her anyway."

"Good, I'll meet you there," he said.

Chapter Eight

Stacy tried to call Tricia.

"She left for the game about fifteen minutes ago," Mrs. Allen said. "May I take a message?"

"Thank you, but that's all right," Stacy replied. She hung up the telephone and turned to her aunt. "I was afraid of that."

"Tricia called while you were out, and I told her about Gary's accident," Aunt Sara said.

"At least she'll know why Andrea's not at the game, but now I don't have a ride, and I just told Drew I'd meet him there. Oh, well," she said, dismissing it with a shrug, "Tricia can explain that I missed her."

"You don't have to break your date," Aunt Sara said. "Jim is taking Hal to the game. You can ride with them."

"Are he and Chris back from hunting?" Stacy asked.

"They came home a little while ago. They went on to the barn to relieve Hal so that he could come home and get ready. Plus, I'm sure Jim wanted to talk to Lane about the accident."

"I guess I should go ahead and go to the game," Stacy said. "I hate to stand Drew up at the last minute."

She started back to her room, and her aunt called after her. "By the way, you got a letter from Philadelphia today. I put it in your room."

Stacy saw the letter on her dresser and recognized Joni's handwriting immediately. She hesitated for a second and then gathered up her robe and headed for the bathroom. If she was going to the game, she had to shower and shampoo her hair, and Aunt Sara had already warned her that Hal would be home soon. In a house with only one bathroom, you had to get your priorities straight, and Stacy had learned the lesson well.

She was just slipping back across the hall when she heard Hal come in through the kitchen. She plugged in her blow dryer and sat down on the bed to read Joni's letter while she dried her hair.

Dear Stacy,
Sorry this thank-you note is so late. I showed everyone the pictures I took in Summerdale, and they all thought Lane was a doll. But we can talk about that later. I want to get right to the good news.

Mom and Dad have planned to go on a Caribbean cruise during the Christmas holidays, so I played on the old heartstrings and got them to agree to let me spend some of the holidays with you! School is out next Friday. With your permission (or I guess I should say—your aunt's permission!) I could fly to Alabama and stay with you until you're ready to return to Philadelphia.

I know you can talk your aunt into it, so call me as soon as possible so that I can make reservations. You know how holiday traffic is.

Love, Joni

Stacy quickly reread the letter. Joni was coming back. Now? That was all she needed.

At Thanksgiving, her friend had made it quite clear that she wasn't impressed with the farm or Summerdale. So why was she making such an effort to come back for only three or four more days?

Lost in thought, Stacy went through the motions of getting dressed for her date. Joni was her oldest friend. They had gone through eleven years of school together. It seemed cold not to want her around, but maybe Joni was right after all—maybe she had changed since her decision to live in Summerdale.

She and Joni had nothing to talk about that didn't begin with, "Remember when..." Maybe one day she'd be nostalgic about her days at the boarding school, but right now she was too busy making new memories.

Her only hope was that Aunt Sara would have some good reason why it wouldn't be practical for Joni to visit them right before Christmas.

As soon as she finished dressing, Stacy went back to the kitchen and found her aunt.

She didn't waste any time getting to the point of Joni's letter.

"It won't be any trouble at all," Aunt Sara said.

"Are you sure?" Stacy asked. "I could arrange to see Joni after I get to Dad's."

Assuming that Smokey was announcing Uncle Jim's arrival, they continued their conversation without paying attention to the dog's barking. "Of course I'm sure. I can put Angie on the cot in our room, and you and Joni can share your room."

The door opened, but it wasn't Uncle Jim who stood there. It was Lane. Stacy took in his dress slacks, neatly pressed blue shirt and sports jacket in one quick glance and turned away. He was obviously on his way to see someone.

He let his eyes slide over Stacy and focused on Sara. "Jim went over to the Broussards' to see if he could help with anything there, and I told him that I'd take Hal to the game. Is he ready?"

"Almost," Aunt Sara said.

Stacy tried to catch her aunt's eye, but she was too late. Aunt Sara was already saying, "Is it all right if Stacy goes with you, too? I promised her that she could ride with Jim and Hal."

"Sure, no problem," Lane said, deliberately keeping his voice impersonal.

As soon as Hal was ready, they said a brief goodbye to Sara, and went out to Lane's car. Hal hung back, so that Stacy was forced to either make a scene and refuse to sit beside Lane or simply go ahead and do it. Of course, the last thing she wanted was for him to know it bothered her. Willing her heart to slow down to a normal rate, she got into the car.

Hal slid in behind her, effectively trapping her between him and Lane. Since there wasn't anything for her to hold on to for support, Stacy tried to compensate for the bounce and sway of the car by leaning toward her cousin, but it didn't help. She couldn't escape the pull of Lane's presence.

Lane broke into her thoughts, saying, "When I came in, Sara was talking about reshuffling bed assignments. Didn't she mention your friend Joni?"

"Yes, she's coming back to visit as soon as school lets out for Christmas vacation."

"Does that mean you'll be staying around here instead of heading back East for Christmas?"

"No. Joni's only coming for a few days, and then she and I will go back to Philadelphia for Christmas."

"Too bad," Lane said.

"I'll tell her you said so," Stacy said.

In the darkened car, Lane couldn't see Stacy's face, and her cool voice gave no hint as to whether she had purposely misinterpreted his question or if she really didn't care that he was interested in someone else. Either way, there wasn't much need for him to say anything else.

After a few minutes of awkward silence, Hal asked Lane about the hunt, and he and Lane began talking about the day and, in general terms, Gary Broussard's accident. Stacy was concentrating so hard on avoiding any unnecessary contact with Lane that she didn't realize they had reached the high school gymnasium until Lane stopped the car.

Lane said, "If you need a lift home, I can . . ."

"Thanks, but I have a ride," Hal said quickly.

"And I have a date," Stacy told him. She had started to slide out of the car after Hal, but Lane stopped her.

"Why didn't he pick you up at home?"

"It's with Drew Riley, and he got tied up helping at the Broussards', so I told him that I'd meet him here," she said. "Why? What did you think?"

"I try not to," he muttered.

He watched until Stacy and Hal were safely inside and then drove away. He'd decided to go to Sheffield where Gary had been transferred. He wanted to be sure that Gary was all right.

He found the Broussard family in one of the waiting rooms of the local hospital. Andrea and Yvette had joined their parents and brother, and Lane could see the relief behind their strained expressions.

"The foot wasn't completely severed. Gary's going to be all right," Mr. Broussard said. "The doctors just finished setting the bones and connecting the tendons and ligaments. They said we'd know if he was going to get any feeling or movement back in the foot in a few days."

"I'm glad to hear that," Lane said.

"We're just grateful that you found him when you did," Mr. Broussard added. "He's in the recovery room now. We're waiting until they take him back to his own room. He probably won't even know we're here, but his mama's going to want to spend the night, anyway."

"I guess I'll go on back home then. If you need anything, I don't mind making another trip."

"No, that's all right, Lane, but we do appreciate the offer," Mrs. Broussard said.

"Since we can't really see Gary tonight, I think I'll go on home," Andrea said. "Lane, would you mind giving me a lift?"

"Of course not. Yvette, you want to come with us?"

Yvette shook her head. "I'll wait with Dad."

"We'll be along in a couple of hours," Mr. Broussard said. "Dan and his wife will be home if Andrea needs anything in the meantime."

Instead of driving directly to Summerdale, Lane detoured through Douglasville. Judging by the number of cars headed toward the Dairy Queen, the basketball game was over, so he suggested they stop by to see who had won.

Andrea was a nice kid, and considering the afternoon and evening she'd had, he figured she deserved a few minutes with her friends. Besides, Stacy might be there with Drew.

Lane didn't see Stacy at first, but she saw him the minute he walked in. Someone tossed an empty cup past the doorway, and Lane threw up his arm to protect Andrea.

Stacy couldn't make out what Andrea said to him, but Lane smiled and hugged her against him as they made their way to a booth behind the one where Stacy was sitting.

Stacy clenched her hands into fists without realizing that she had crushed her straw, and Drew passed her another one. "We can leave if you want to," he said quietly.

They were sitting beside Bobby Hall with Tricia, Regina Dawson, and Marsh Compton across the table from them, so Stacy kept her voice so low that Drew had to lean closer to hear her. "I can take it if you can," she said.

"What do you mean?" he asked.

"Doesn't it bother you?" When she realized that Drew didn't have the slightest idea what she was talking about, she stopped and started over. "I'm sorry. I heard that you liked Andrea."

Drew shook his head. "No, but don't get me wrong. I was interested in her for a while, but she's having too much fun playing the field. I don't think she's ready for anything serious yet."

"She looks pretty serious to me," Stacy said. She had sneaked a peek in their direction and saw Lane's arm curved around the top of the booth with Andrea cradled next to his side.

Over the noise of the crowd, someone asked Andrea about her brother, and everyone stopped to listen to her answer.

"We just came from the hospital," she said, touching Lane's shoulder. "He just came out of one operation, and the doctor thinks he's going to be all right."

At the sound of Andrea's voice, Tricia glanced over her shoulder, and when she looked back at Stacy, her eyes were as big as saucers. "Uh, do you want to try to see if we can make it through this crowd to the bathroom?" she asked.

"If we can figure out how to get out of this booth," Stacy said.

Everyone had to stand up and switch places, but the girls finally got out. As soon as she could talk without worrying whether she would be overheard, Tricia whispered, "When did they come in?"

"A few minutes ago," Stacy said.

"You knew they were there all the while?"

Stacy nodded, and Tricia said, "I had no idea. You really hid it well."

"Thanks," Stacy said dryly. "Now do you want to tell me again that last Saturday night was just a coincidence."

"I don't know what to think," Tricia said. "Just be careful. Don't let anyone else know there's anything wrong."

Stacy raised her voice so that anyone listening could hear her. "By the way, I got a letter from Joni today. She's coming back for another visit. She'll be here next Friday."

"I didn't think she cared much for our rural life-style," Tricia said.

"I don't think it's the life-style that's caught her attention."

"What about the Christmas dance? You and I are supposed to double-date."

"I know."

"Do you want me to see if Chuck has a friend he can bring home for her, too?"

"Thanks, but it's not fair to ask Chuck to supply more than one other date. Besides, I have another idea for Joni."

When they got back to their table, Stacy tried to concentrate on Drew and ignore the way Andrea was hanging on to Lane's arm. Still, she was acutely aware when they left. She and Drew followed a few minutes later.

On the way home Drew said, "Do you mind if I ask why you accepted a date with me? I know a couple of other guys were planning to call you."

"I thought I would have more fun if I went out with a friend," Stacy said.

"So much for my roguish charm," Drew said with a grin.

"I didn't mean that. You're very charming," Stacy told him. "So much so that I wanted to ask you about taking Joni out again."

"She's coming back?"

Stacy nodded. "And I need to get her a date for the Christmas dance."

"I'd be happy to take her if I'm still here."

"What do you mean?" Stacy asked.

"We haven't told many people, but the reason I haven't asked anyone to the dance is because I'm not exactly sure what my mother's plans are. See, she's getting married right after Christmas, and—"

"Drew, I had no idea! Who's she marrying?"

"No one from around here. Actually he's from Pittsburgh."

"Do you like him?"

"Yeah, he seems all right, but I'd appreciate it if you didn't tell anyone. Mom's trying to keep it quiet."

"I won't tell, but if Aunt Sara finds out that I knew something this good and didn't tell her, she won't let me have any dessert for a week." Stacy laughed.

When they reached her aunt's house, Drew said, "I'll talk to Mom tomorrow and see if we're going to be around for the Christmas dance. If I find out that I can't take Joni, I'll help you come up with another date for her."

"Thanks, Drew, I'd really appreciate it," Stacy said.

She was still smiling when she went inside. Drew was so nice. She was glad she had decided to take Tricia's advice and go out with him. She felt so much better, she didn't even dread Joni's visit. If it hadn't been so late, she would have called Joni right then, but considering the time, she wisely decided to wait until after church the next day.

Joni answered on the first ring. "I was wondering if you'd gotten my letter," she said breathlessly.

"It came yesterday, but things were a little hectic around here. One of our neighbors was hurt in an accident, so I had to run some errands for them. Then, by the time I got home last night, it was too late to call you."

"I suppose you were out with Lane," Joni said.

"I was out, but not with Lane."

There was a long pause before Joni asked, "What do you mean?"

"Lane and I've broken up."

"Why? What happened?"

"It's too long of a story to get into now. I'll tell you all about it when you get here."

"Then it is all right for me to come?"

"Yes, of course. I should have told you that right away. I spoke to Aunt Sara, and she said it was fine."

"Then I'll call the airlines and get the earliest flight out of here on Friday. Will someone meet me in Sheffield or should I take a taxi out to your aunt's?"

"A bus maybe, but you won't find a taxi," Stacy said. "Don't worry about it though, we'll get you here somehow. And be sure to bring something to wear to a dance Saturday night."

"A dance? Does this mean that you're going to set me up with a date?"

"I did all right with the last one, didn't I?"

"Yes, but what about Lane? If you and he have really broken up, I wouldn't mind going out with him."

Everything got quiet. Even Stacy's heart stopped beating. If Joni was teasing, she didn't think it was very funny.

"I wouldn't count on going out with Lane if I were you," Stacy finally said. "He was out with Andrea Broussard tonight."

"But you're sure you two are really through?"

"Yes, I'm sure."

"Well, what do you know. I may enjoy this trip more than I thought." When Stacy didn't reply, Joni asked, "Is everything all right?"

"Everything's fine," Stacy managed to say. "I'll see you on Friday."

Chapter Nine

Stacy told herself that it got a little easier every day. She stopped waiting for Lane to call, and she only went to the dairy if she was certain that he wouldn't be there. When she couldn't avoid him, she was all right as long as she kept busy and didn't meet his eyes.

Because everyone at school was getting ready for Christmas vacation, no one had his or her mind on work. Even the teachers let up on their assignments. With more time on her hands, Stacy had time to think about her future. She even scheduled an appointment with the school guidance counselor for some advice about colleges.

On Friday, Sara went into Sheffield to do some Christmas shopping and arranged to meet Joni's plane. And since her aunt had their car, Stacy and her cousins rode home from school that afternoon with Tricia and her little sister.

All six of them, with their books, jackets, and assorted Christmas presents, crammed into one car made it very crowded, but no one really cared. It was Christmas, and they were beginning a two-week vacation from school. All the way home, Hal and Chris entertained them with some new words to some of the old, familiar Christmas carols.

"You sound as though you're glad to be out of school," Aunt Sara said when she heard them coming in.

"Not me," Chris insisted. "I cried when the last bell rang."

"That's because Mrs. Johnson told you the Christmas party was over, and you'd have to stop eating," Hal said, poking him in the ribs.

Stacy caught her aunt's eye and over the noise of her cousins' scuffle, she asked, "Where's Joni? She didn't miss her plane, did she?"

"No, nothing like that. She's at the barn with Lane. He came by just as we got home, and she insisted on going to the dairy to help him. You don't have to tell her he said so, but Lane left word that he wanted some *real* help as soon as y'all got home from school."

Stacy sighed. "I'll get changed and go help," she said. "After all, Joni's my guest, so I guess that makes her my responsibility." She reminded herself that she expected something like this to happen. Joni hadn't been exactly shy about her attraction to Lane, and now that they had broken up... She didn't even want to think about it.

She had left her boots in the washroom, so after she changed clothes, she pulled on a pair of thick socks and padded out to get them.

"It's cold out there today, so be sure to take a jacket," her aunt told her. "When Jim comes in, we're all going out in the pasture to find a Christmas tree. We'll decorate it after dinner tonight."

"Tell Joni she can help us," Angie said.

"I'm sure she'll like that," Stacy said, ruffling Angie's hair and heading out to the truck.

She drove over to the dairy, and before she brought the pickup to a full stop, she saw Joni standing in the doorway. Joni was wearing designer jeans, high-heeled boots, a denim vest with thick lamb's-wool lining and a white sweater. Stacy was sure the outfit hadn't been designed for wear at a dairy, but Joni looked fabulous. She felt small and drab by comparison.

Joni put her hands on her hips, and when Stacy got out of the truck, she asked, "Now who's the real country girl?"

Behind her, Lane almost dropped the milking machine he was moving. Joni couldn't see him, but Stacy did, and she laughed. "Not you, that's for sure," she said, walking up and hugging her friend. "Have you really been helping?"

"Of course, this is a real two-man operation."

Before Stacy could comment on the marked difference between Lane's clothes and Joni's spotless ones, Lane called out "Heads up!"

Stacy realized that he was ready to release the first group of cows and automatically pulled Joni out of the way. Without waiting to see if Joni was going to follow her, Stacy hurried over to the feed trough and began putting out feed for the next cows.

As the cows came into the barn, Lane moved down the line, locking them into place. Stacy followed him with the disinfectant, cleaning each cow's udder before he put the milking machines in place. They worked well together, their rhythm returning as though there had never been an interruption.

As soon as she could, Stacy rejoined Joni at the window.

"By the way, did you get me a date for that dance you mentioned?" Joni asked.

Stacy nodded. "I asked Drew. I would have told you when I called, but he had to check with his mother's plans. See, she's getting remarried and—"

Joni interrupted her. "Could you get me out of it?"

"Why? The dance is tomorrow night."

"Yes, but—" Joni let her gaze wander to Lane before she finished "—I, uh, got my own date."

Stacy forced herself to continue breathing at a normal rate but words were impossible.

"It's all right, isn't it?" Joni continued. "When I mentioned it on the telephone, you didn't say I shouldn't—you just said he'd probably be out with that Broussard girl."

"Andrea," Stacy supplied. "I thought he would, but that's not the point. What am I going to tell Drew?"

"You'll think of something. Why don't we go back to your aunt's and maybe we can..."

"Someone has to help Lane," Stacy said. "It was your idea to come out here in the first place, remember?"

A cow flicked her tail, and Joni held her hands up in front of her face. "Well, can't you at least tie down their tails or something?"

"Just try to keep out of the way until we're through," Stacy said.

At the next break, when the milking machines were again in place, Joni asked, "What have you got planned for tonight? Are we going out somewhere?"

"No, we're going to help decorate our Christmas tree."

"Is Lane coming?" Joni asked.

"I don't know what he's doing," Stacy said.

"Well, let's ask him."

Before Stacy could stop her, Joni raised her voice and called to Lane. "How do you feel about decorating?"

"Decorating?" he asked.

"You know, Christmas trees," Joni said. "Ornaments, tinsel and my personal favorite—mistletoe. You want to help us?"

"He probably has to help his grandmother," Stacy said.

"I brought her tree home before I came to the barn," Lane said. "She's probably finished decorating it by now."

"You didn't help her?" Stacy asked.

"She's been doing it long enough. I figure she knows how she wants it done."

They were interrupted by the sound of the station wagon pulling up in front of the barn. Uncle Jim, Aunt Sara, Angie, Chris and Hal all poured out.

"Come on! We're going to get our Christmas tree," Angie called.

"I can't. We're not through milking," Stacy said.

"That's all right," Hal said. "You and Joni can go. I'll stay and help Lane."

Joni didn't need a second invitation. She was already heading toward the station wagon when Jim stopped her.

"We'll take the truck to get the tree. Hal can bring the car home when he's through here."

Joni followed Sara into the truck cab, but Stacy held back. "Uncle Jim, is it all right if I go to Mrs. Kate's and see if I can help her with her tree? I'll catch a ride home with Hal."

"Sure, if that's what you want to do," he said. "We'll see you at home later."

Stacy waved as they drove away and then walked to Mrs. Colby's. According to Lane, she should be through with her tree by now, but Stacy didn't see Christmas lights from any of the windows. With the familiarity of someone who knew her way around, Stacy went around to the back door and let herself in, calling out as she did.

"Is something wrong?" Mrs. Colby asked.

It was Mrs. Colby's habit to get straight to the point, so Stacy did, too. "No, but Lane mentioned that you were decorating your Christmas tree. I wondered if you could use some help."

Mrs. Colby didn't smile, but the firm line of her mouth softened. "It doesn't usually take me this long, but I'm having trouble with the lights," she said, leading the way into the living room.

The tree was standing in front of the double windows but the lights were stretched out across the floor. "With these lights, if one bulb burns out or gets loose, it breaks the circuit and none of the lights will work."

"My mother told me about these," Stacy said. "Can't you just replace the bad bulb?"

"First you have to find it," Mrs. Colby said. "I've gone over the entire string and checked each bulb, but I couldn't find any that looked bad. The only thing to do now is to try a new bulb in each socket until we find the culprit."

"What if the new bulb is bad? Or if you have two..."

"Hush," Mrs. Colby said sharply. "Don't borrow trouble. Just stand over there by the wall socket and plug in the string when I tell you to."

It took them the rest of the hour to work through the string and find the bad bulb. Once the circuit was completed the floor glowed with lights of deep lustrous color.

Mrs. Colby sighed. "Finally. Every year I keep saying I'm going to replace these with the new kind. This might be their last year."

"I don't know," Stacy said. "When you finally get these lit, you feel as though you've really accomplished something."

"Yes, but it's getting harder and harder to get replacement bulbs."

While they talked, they each took one end of the string of lights and began spacing them evenly around the tree. After they were satisfied with the placement, Mrs. Colby went to get the ornaments.

Stacy picked up bits of cedar that had fallen from the tree and tossed them into the fire. Standing before the fireplace, she noticed for the first time that the rack of deer antlers over the fireplace had been replaced by a large wooden and brass clock.

She was still staring at it when Mrs. Colby returned. "When did you get that?" she asked.

"Lane bought it last week. He said it was an early Christmas present."

She set the box of ornaments in front of the tree and said, "Some of these are so old, I don't even know how they'll look."

"I don't know what Mother did with our ornaments after we took them off the tree," Stacy said. "It seems that we had different ones every year. One year everything was in blue, then white, and silver."

"I probably should buy some new decorations myself. I never did replace the ones I lost the year Lane got a basketball for Christmas," Mrs. Colby said.

They worked together companionably, with Mrs. Colby recounting the family's history, Christmas by Christmas, until the box was empty. Stacy picked up the last ornament, a small silver bell trimmed with a delicate silver bow. "Oh, this is beautiful," she said.

"Lane's mother bought that the year she was married," Mrs. Colby said. "I always leave it until last because it has to be polished before it can be hung. With the way my eyes are, I don't know if it's worth the trouble."

"I'll polish it for you," Stacy said.

"You go right ahead. I'll make us some hot chocolate."

Stacy got the silver polish and went back to the living room to enjoy the glow of the tree while she worked. When she finished, she held the bell up for inspection and saw Lane standing in the doorway, watching her.

"What are you doing here?" he asked.

Stacy jerked her arm down guiltily and then realized that she hadn't done anything wrong. "Helping your grandmother decorate her tree," she said. "We'll be through as soon as I find a place for this."

"Here, let me," he said, taking the little bell from her nerveless fingers. He placed it high on the tree where it reflected the glow of the colored lights.

"It's beautiful," Stacy murmured. She glanced over at Lane and discovered that he was watching her, his gaze as soft as a caress.

Her heart lurched wildly, and she searched for something to say. "I like the clock you gave your grandmother."

The corner of Lane's mouth started to curve into a smile, but he quickly brought it back under control. "That doesn't mean I've changed my mind about deer hunting," he said.

Stacy didn't say anything, but her heart felt lighter than it had in weeks.

"The chocolate's ready," Mrs. Colby said coming into the room with a tray and two cups.

Suddenly anxious to get away, Stacy picked up her jacket and started for the kitchen. "Thanks, but I'm afraid I can't stay after all. I'll have to hurry if I'm going to catch a ride home with Hal."

"Hal's already left," Lane said. "Give me a few minutes to clean up, and I'll take you."

"That's all right. I'll call Hal at home. He won't mind coming back for me."

"But I do. He doesn't need to be running up and down the highway at all hours of the night."

To get to his grandmother's from home, Hal would be on the highway for less than five minutes, and it was only around seven. But it didn't matter. Lane's attitude didn't invite any argument, so Stacy gave in, took a cup of chocolate and sat down to wait.

Lane didn't take very long, and when he was ready to leave, Stacy invited Mrs. Colby to join them.

"I'm going to turn in early tonight," Mrs. Colby said. "Tell Sara I'll come by to see her tree tomorrow."

Waiting for Stacy to say good-night to his grandmother, Lane let himself forget what had happened between them. For a minute, it seemed just like old times. He jammed his fists into his jacket pockets to keep from reaching for her when they walked out to his car.

Once they were on their way, Stacy broke the spell by saying, "I guess I should thank you for agreeing to take Joni to the dance."

"Glad I could help," he said shortly.

He hadn't wanted her gratitude. He wanted her to feel the same way he did when he knew she was out on a date. She hadn't even looked up when he stopped by the Dairy Queen with Andrea Broussard, but he'd counted on his date with Joni causing some kind of reaction.

He sneaked a glance at her but she was staring straight ahead at the road. They drove the rest of the way in silence.

By the time they got to the house, they found Uncle Jim and Hal had finished making a stand for the Christmas tree and were busy placing it in the corner beside the fireplace. Much larger than Mrs. Colby's, the tree filled the entire corner and the fresh cedar scent permeated the room.

"Think you got one big enough?" Lane asked.

"I picked it out," Chris said proudly. "I found it two years ago, and I've been watching it ever since."

Aunt Sara finished arranging a buffet of cold cuts and fresh fruit on the table and said, "Everyone have something to eat before we start decorating."

"The rest of you go ahead," Stacy said. "I'll change and be back in a minute."

Joni had already changed into a clinging red jumpsuit, and Stacy had no intention of staying in her dirty jeans. Still, she didn't want to appear to be competing with her friend, so after a quick bath she discarded her dirty jeans for a pair of clean ones. She did, however, choose a soft blue pullover sweater and add a touch of her best cologne, Lane's favorite.

When she got back to the living room, Uncle Jim and Lane were already putting the last string of lights on the tree.

"I remember when it used to take us half the night just to get this far," Jim said. "First we had to find out if the lights were working, and if they weren't, we had to figure out which one had burned out."

"Grandma still uses that kind," Lane said.

"That's what took us so long to finish her tree tonight," Stacy said.

Sara handed Stacy a plate that had been fixed for her, and Stacy sat down at the counter to eat. She noticed that Joni had stationed herself beside Lane so that her shoulder brushed against him as she handed him ornaments to hang on the tree.

"Before I left school, each class was responsible for decorating the entrance hall to one of the main buildings," Joni said. "Afterward, we had a contest to see which one was the prettiest, and naturally, the seniors won."

"If I remember correctly, the seniors always judged that contest," Stacy said.

"I know, but we did have the prettiest display," Joni insisted. "When we get home, we'll go by the school and you can see for yourself—if we have time, that is.

We've got invitations to at least twenty parties between Christmas and New Year's Day."

"We have Christmas parties here, too," Angie said. "Are you coming to our party, Stacy?"

"I don't know, sweetie. When's it going to be?" Stacy asked.

"She means the one at the community center," Sara said. "It's Sunday night after the regular church service. When's your father expecting you?"

"Dad made the reservations," Stacy said. "I think they're—"

"Monday," Joni supplied. "At least that's what he told my grandmother. She's picking us up at the airport."

"I thought your family was going to be away," Stacy said.

"Not my grandmother. I'll be staying with her when I'm not with you. But don't worry, she doesn't live very far from your Dad."

"Will you be here for our party?" Angie asked again.

"I wouldn't miss it," Stacy said. "Is Santa Claus going to be there?"

Angie hesitated. She didn't want her brothers teasing her, but Santa's arrival was her favorite part of the party.

"Yeah, Angie, is Santa Claus going to pop out of the chimney and give everyone presents?" Chris asked.

"He came last year," Angie said.

"But he didn't come down the chimney," Hal said. "He walked in the door just like...just like Mr. Dawson would have—if he'd been there. You know, I still wonder why he didn't come. The rest of his family was there."

Stacy interrupted them. "Hal, will you and Chris go get the presents I hid in my closet?"

"Are any of them for us?" Chris asked.

"Let me put it this way," Stacy threatened, "not if you two don't stop teasing Angie."

Sara called Angie away to help her with their gifts, and when the little girl was out of the room, Lane said, "She's six years old. She's going to have to learn the truth eventually."

"Not now," Stacy said. "Christmas is only a few days away. It won't hurt to pretend for a little while longer."

They were only a few feet apart, and Lane's eyes caught hers and held them. "Sometimes it's better to go ahead and face the facts instead of hiding from them," he said.

Hal and Chris returned with an armful of gifts, and for once they were too distracted by the strange shapes and rattles of the packages to continue teasing their sister, who was busy trying to find gifts with her name on them.

Aware that the tension between Lane and Stacy had nothing to do with Santa, Joni tried to change the subject. "You know what we need to complete the decorations? Some mistletoe."

"I put some in the back of the truck," Chris said. "I'll go get it."

Chapter Ten

Without saying anything to anyone, Stacy slipped back to her room before Chris returned with the mistletoe. She had no intention of throwing herself on the bed and giving in to her feelings, and it was just as well. Joni hadn't unpacked, but she'd left her suitcases open on the bed.

Just to have something to do, Stacy began putting the clothes away. She had finished the first suitcase when Joni came in.

"Why did you leave?" Joni asked.

"I thought I should make room in my closet for your things," Stacy said. "We can't have you living out of your suitcase until Monday."

Joni made herself comfortable on the bed, obviously not in any hurry to return to the family room, and Stacy asked, "Is everyone else getting ready to go to bed?"

"Your cousins are, but I think your aunt and uncle are still up," Joni said. "Lane left right after you did. That's why I decided to come on in here."

Joni waited, and when Stacy didn't comment, she asked, "Is anything wrong? You've hardly spoken to me since I arrived."

"No, nothing's wrong," Stacy said. "You were at the barn when I got home from school, and I went over to Mrs. Colby's because I thought someone should help her with her tree."

"I thought it might have something to do with Lane. It is over between you two, isn't it?"

Stacy raised her eyebrows. She couldn't help it. "Isn't it a little late to be asking that?"

"Oh? You mean I should have checked with you *before* I got him to ask me to that dance? Look, if it bothers you, I'll..."

"No," Stacy said, instantly contrite. "It's all right. I have a date to the dance, so why shouldn't he?"

"Who are you going with?" Joni asked.

"Tricia's boyfriend set me up with his roommate from college. I haven't met him yet, but Chuck has assured Tricia that he's nice."

"You know, you still haven't told me why you and Lane broke up."

"We just did, that's all," Stacy said. "It doesn't really matter why. I'm just glad that something good came out of it."

"Then you're glad it's over?"

Stacy hedged. She wouldn't go that far. "When you and Mom were here at Thanksgiving, Mom implied that Lane was the only reason I wanted to stay here."

"You have to admit that he is a pretty big incentive," Joni said.

Stacy made a face. "Aren't you the one who said we shouldn't plan our future around getting married? Since Lane and I broke up, I've had plenty of time to think about what I wanted to do with my life."

"And?"

"I don't know if you'll understand—I don't even know if Mom or Dad will—but this is my home. I'll visit Philadelphia and Washington, but this is where I want to live."

"What about college?"

"There are colleges in Alabama. I've already talked to the counselor at school. She's helping me decide where I should apply."

"I thought we were going to be roommates," Joni said.

"That's still possible. All you have to do is transfer to a college in Alabama."

"I'll think about it," Joni said. "I'll let you know after my date tomorrow night."

When Joni got up the next morning, Stacy was outside saddling her horse.

"Where are we going?" Joni asked.

"*We* aren't," Stacy said. "I am."

"Oh?"

Stacy smiled. "I'm going over to the Broussards'. Drew's been working there regularly since Gary Broussard's accident. I thought I'd go ahead and tell him that you already have a date for tonight. Of course, if you want to come with me..."

"That's all right. I'll let you handle it. You know Drew better than I do," Joni said. "You'll know what to say to him."

Actually Stacy wanted to go alone. There was more at stake than just breaking Joni's date. She couldn't remember who started it, but someone had spread the word that Andrea had a date with Lane for the Christmas dance. Was that just what Andrea wanted everyone to think, or did she really believe it herself?

Stacy gave her horse his head and enjoyed a brisk ride through the pastures to the Broussards' farm. She went around to the back and headed straight for the corral. Drew was there, but so was Yvette.

After a minute's hesitation, Stacy realized it might be for the best. Time was running out, and she needed some inside information, fast.

"I know this may sound crazy, but Yvette, I have to know the truth. Who's taking Andrea to the Christmas dance?"

Yvette glanced from Stacy to Drew and back. She was clearly uncomfortable, but she didn't avoid the question. "Lane. It's all right, isn't it? I mean, you two—"

Stacy cut her off. "I was afraid of that," she said, and sat down with a sigh. "We've got a problem, and it's going to take all of us to figure out what to do about it."

"What is it?" Drew asked. "Have you and Lane made up?"

"No, it doesn't have anything to do with me," Stacy said. "Joni arrived before I got home from school yesterday, and before I had a chance to see her and tell her that I had arranged for you to take her to the dance, she accepted a date with Lane."

"Lane? Are you sure?" Yvette asked.

Stacy nodded. "Joni told me, and when I mentioned it to Lane later, he confirmed it."

"Did he say anything about Andrea?" Drew asked.

"No, but I didn't ask. At the moment I was more concerned about what I was going to say to you. I didn't even think about Andrea until this morning."

"Andrea still thinks she has a date with Lane," Yvette said. "She mentioned it this morning."

"I don't know what's happened," Stacy said. "I know Andrea doesn't have to pretend she has a date with anyone, but Lane just isn't the type to stand anyone up, either."

"Well, since I'm fresh out of a date, I'd be glad to take Andrea. Of course, I don't know if she would go with me," Drew said.

Yvette made an unladylike sound. "If you tell her why you're asking her, I guarantee you she won't. The thing is—plenty of boys asked her, but she turned them all down."

"Did she tell them that she had a date with Lane?"

"I don't think so," Yvette said. "I think she was keeping them guessing. She just said something vague about already having plans."

"Drew, what if you told her that you heard she'd dropped Lane and then asked her if she'd go with you."

"Well, you know she's going to ask where I heard something like that. What do I say?"

Stacy paused. "You're going to have to word it carefully. Something like...you know Lane has a date with Joni, so you figured that if he was getting a date, no, make that... *another* date—if he was getting another date at the last minute, it must be because she broke up with him."

"That might work," Yvette said. "Especially if you ask her before anyone else hears about Lane and Joni."

"I'll go up to the house and ask her now," Drew said.

"Let me get out of here first," Stacy said. "One of you can let me know what happens later. If we have to, we can still go to Lane and explain it to him."

"I'll call you," Yvette said. "And thanks. If Andrea knew what you were doing for her..."

"I don't think we'd better tell her, at least not now," Stacy said.

"You're probably right," Yvette agreed. "If she had any idea that we had to fix her up with a date at the last minute, she'd refuse to go at all—I don't care how much she wants to be Sweetheart."

Stacy left the way she'd come, but she detoured by Tricia's before going back home. Tricia was the only other person she had told about getting Joni a date with Drew, and she wanted to let her know about the change in plans.

"Wait, let me get this straight," Tricia said after Stacy had finished the story. "Your ex-boyfriend asked your best friend for a date, so you took it on yourself to see that the other girl he's been dating has a date, too."

"I know it sounds strange, but can you imagine how Andrea would have felt after getting all dressed up for a big dance and then her date not showing up? I couldn't just stand by and let that happen."

"That would have been horrible," Tricia said. "Especially in a town like Douglasville. She'd never be able to live it down completely. But why didn't you just tell Lane? If he knew Andrea thought she had a date with him, I'm sure he would have gone with her and Joni could have still gone with Drew."

"Well, I didn't know for sure that Andrea thought she had a date with Lane until I talked to Yvette this morning. And Joni really wants to go with Lane. Knowing her, she might have mentioned the switch in dates to Andrea," Stacy said, and then continued sheepishly. "Besides, Lane and I argued about Joni the night we broke up. I don't want him to think I'm trying to keep him from going out with her. He might get the idea that I'm jealous."

"Are you?"

Stacy changed the subject. "Have you heard from my date yet?"

"He has a name, Stacy," Tricia said. "Ken Bilderback, remember? And yes, Chuck called this morning. He and Ken got in late last night."

"I'm glad they got here all right, but frankly, I wish this whole thing was already over. I'm not looking forward to being there when Lane comes to pick up his date tonight."

"I can help you with that," Tricia said. "I have to be at the dance early, so we should be there to get you before Lane comes for Joni."

"I'd appreciate that," Stacy said. "Now I'd better get home before Aunt Sara and Joni start wondering about what's happened to me."

Back at home, Stacy stayed near the telephone until Yvette called to let her know that Andrea had accepted Drew's offer. Afterward, she and Joni ran into Douglasville on an errand for Aunt Sara and then spent the rest of the afternoon wandering about the farm and talking.

After an early dinner, they started getting ready for the dance. Joni took out a black-and-white dress and left it on the bed while she worked on her hair and makeup, but knowing that Tricia had promised to be there early, Stacy dressed quickly.

She had chosen a royal-blue dress with long sleeves and a high cowl neckline that dipped low, almost to her waist, in the back. The full skirt swirled around her knees. She was putting on her lipstick when she heard Smokey barking.

"That's probably my date," Stacy said. "Do you want me to keep him here until you can meet him?"

"No, that's okay. I'll be a while yet. I want everyone to sit up and take notice when I walk into the dance," Joni said.

"I'll try to prepare them for you," Stacy said, picking up her evening bag. "See you there."

In the family room, Tricia, looking lovely in a pale pink dress, was standing between Chuck Hastings and one of the best-looking boys Stacy had seen in a long time. Tall, with a good build, thick brown hair and nice hazel eyes, Ken Bilderback seemed perfectly at ease with her aunt and uncle. Of course, with his looks, he probably met a lot of parents, Stacy reasoned.

Chuck made the introductions, and Tricia explained to Stacy's aunt and uncle that they had to get to the dance early. Helped along by Tricia and Chuck, the conversation on the way to school was easy and natural. Stacy learned that Ken had a younger brother at home, he was studying engineering and he had a pleasant sense of humor. By the time they all reached the auditorium Stacy felt quite at home with him.

Since the close of school on Friday afternoon, the combination cafeteria-auditorium had been transformed with artificial snow, cotton batting and twinkling white lights into a glittering winter wonderland. The tables were covered with white tablecloths and decorated with poinsettias and candles. Two large Christmas trees adorned either side of the small stage.

It seemed strange to Stacy to be at such an occasion without Lane at her side. Other couples, with girls who were on the new court or, like Tricia, part of the outgoing one, were already there. Stacy could feel their eyes on her as she and Ken walked across the room to claim a table near the stage.

Tricia and Chuck excused themselves so that Tricia could find out what she was supposed to do in the lead-out, and for the first time, Stacy was alone with Ken.

"Why aren't you up there with the other girls?" he asked.

"You have to be elected to the court as a junior. I didn't live here then."

"Really? I thought you were a hometown girl."

"I am now," she said proudly, smiling at his confusion. She started to explain what she meant, and then Ken talked about his hometown. Although they were deep in conversation, Stacy could feel the sudden electricity in the room when Lane and Joni entered.

She knew Joni enjoyed the attention she attracted as she walked across the room. The strapless dress with the black bodice and layers of white ruffles on the skirt was even more eye-catching on her than it had been lying on the bed. Her dark hair was pulled back from her face and fastened at her nape with a large bow, adding to her sophisticated, glamorous look.

Until that minute Stacy hadn't realized the full extent of what Joni's date with Lane would mean. She hadn't counted on them sitting at her table, but that was exactly where Joni was headed. There was no way she could refuse to let her friend join them, so as graciously as possible, she introduced Joni and Lane to Ken and then turned her attention to the girls on stage.

The cafeteria was filling up quickly now. Every table was already full, and parents, relatives, and even teachers crowded along the walls. The Key Club members and their dates had assembled for the traditional lead-out, and the room was buzzing with excitement.

"Is the whole town coming to this thing?" Joni asked.

"Most of the spectators will leave after they've introduced the new court and announced the new Sweetheart," Stacy said.

The five junior girls of the new court were introduced last, and from the crowd's reaction, it was easy to tell that Andrea was the favorite. No one was surprised when she was named the new Sweetheart. Tricia presented her with a bouquet of roses, and then waited with the rest of the Key Club members while Andrea and Drew led the first dance.

Stacy was relieved when the next song began and Ken asked her to dance. Keeping her eyes off Lane and Joni was proving more difficult than she had thought it would be. Ken was a smooth dancer, with the extra dash of someone who had worked at his style, and after a few minutes, Stacy began to relax.

She almost missed Ken's question. "Who was it you just broke up with?"

"How did you know? Did Chuck say something?"

"No, I just figured there had to be a good reason a girl as pretty as you are didn't have a date to one of these things."

"I guess I should have told you myself. I didn't mean you to think I was using you."

"No problem. I was promised a beautiful date, and that's what I got."

Stacy smiled her appreciation. "Do you have a girlfriend at home?"

"I've been dating someone, but not exclusively."

"I'm glad. I'd hate to think someone was being hurt by this."

"Is your ex-boyfriend here?"

"Does it show?"

"Not really, but if I had to guess, I'd narrow it down to two possibilities."

"Really? Who?"

"Was it the guy who was in the lead-out with the new Sweetheart? I thought I saw you two smiling at each other."

"No, that's Drew Riley. He's just a good friend."

"Then it's the big, blond guy," Ken said. "With my luck, I should have guessed him first."

"Lane? Why?"

"He's been glaring at me ever since he came in. With the name of Colby, I was hoping he was a relative."

"He's not, but there's no reason for him to be upset with you. He thought we should stop seeing each other."

"That's funny. He doesn't look stupid," Ken said.

Stacy smiled. "Thanks, Ken."

She felt someone tap her shoulder and turned around to see Joni smiling at her.

"I think you two should know the music's stopped," Joni said.

Ken chuckled, and Stacy gave a small embarrassed giggle as they realized that most of the other couples had already made it off the floor.

Lane turned away, and Ken whispered to Stacy, "I don't care what you say—that was a glare."

Stacy couldn't stop the small spark of hope. Was it possible? Lane did look angry. But why? He couldn't be jealous, could he?

Andrea and Drew had joined their table, and there was a crowd of people around still congratulating Andrea. Joni made a fuss over Drew and pulled him away to the dance floor. When the crowd began to thin out, Lane said, "Andrea, I think you promised me a dance."

As soon as they left, Tricia sent Chuck and Ken after some punch, and asked Stacy, "What was going on between you and Ken on the dance floor?"

"Nothing. We were just talking. Why?"

Tricia said, "Chuck says Lane looks as if he's going to explode."

"Really?" Stacy asked.

"You don't have to look so pleased. Since Ken is his roommate, Chuck's afraid Lane may take it out on him."

Andrea walked up with Drew, and Stacy asked, "Where's Joni?"

Andrea shrugged. "Oh, she and Lane left. She said to tell you that she'd see you back at your aunt's."

Stacy muttered to Tricia, "He was really upset all right. He probably couldn't wait to get Joni all to himself!"

"You don't know that," Tricia reminded her. "Just try to enjoy the rest of the dance."

Ken made it easier for Stacy to put Lane out of her mind for a little while, and since Tricia and Chuck wanted some time alone, and Ken had to get up early to catch a plane for Chicago, they didn't stay until the end of the dance themselves.

Stacy was surprised to find that Joni had beaten her home and was just slipping into bed. "Why did you and Lane leave early?" she couldn't resist asking.

"I got Lane to take me to that little...club we went to at Thanksgiving. I thought it might cheer him up, but it was dead tonight. Everyone in town must have been at school. I'll be glad when we go home."

"Why? I thought you wanted to come?"

"I know, but I just realized that I miss the holiday crowds with everyone rushing around."

"People in Summerdale rush, too."

"Why? There's nowhere to go!"

"Sure there is. Don't forget we're going to the community Christmas party tomorrow night. You don't mind, do you?"

"No, I guess not. I did have a good time with your friends at Thanksgiving. I probably would have had a better time tonight if I had gone to the dance with Drew instead of Lane."

"Why do you say that?"

"Lane was nice enough, but I got the impression he was just going through the motions. I don't even know why I ever thought I was attracted to the strong, silent type."

Stacy turned away. She didn't want Joni to see the smile she just couldn't suppress.

Chapter Eleven

The idea that had been forming in Stacy's mind took shape during church service the next morning. As soon as they got home, she had a brief conversation with her aunt and then made two telephone calls. The second one was to her father.

Concern was evident in his voice as soon as he recognized hers. "Is everything all right?"

"Yes, of course, Dad," she said. "I...I just wanted to know what plans you made for Christmas Eve."

There was a slight hesitation before her father said, "Well, we've been invited to have dinner with a friend of mine. She's a very nice lady, and she has twin daughters just a few years younger than you."

"Would there be any problem with the invitation if I weren't there?" Stacy asked.

"Where would you be?" her father asked. "I know you'll want to spend time with your own friends, but

I didn't think you'd start making dates before you even got here."

"It's not anything like that," Stacy said. "I just want to stay at Aunt Sara's through Christmas Eve. Would you mind?"

"This isn't because you don't want to meet my friend, is it? If you would rather that we spend the evening alone, I'm sure that Adrienne would understand."

"Oh, no, I'm glad you have plans. If I thought you were going to be alone, I'd never ask to stay, but if it's all right, I'd like to be with Angie, Hal and Chris on Christmas morning. Could I, Dad?"

"Airlines are usually booked well in advance of the holidays," her father replied.

"That's why I called the airline before I called you. They do have seats available on Christmas Day. I could have breakfast in Alabama and dinner with you in Pennsylvania."

"All right, then. I'll go ahead and make the arrangements. You can change your ticket when you take Joni to the airport tomorrow."

"Thanks, Dad, and Merry Christmas," she added before hanging up. Now all she had to do was tell Joni.

She found her friend in their room, sorting through her clothes, and broke the news of her plans as gently as possible.

Joni shrugged. "I can't say that I'm surprised. I'd have to be blind not to have seen this coming," she said.

"Then you do understand?"

"I won't go that far, but if it's what you want, it's fine with me. There is one thing you can tell me, though."

"What's that?"

"What should I wear to the community party tonight?"

Stacy laughed. One thing you could always count on from Joni. She never wasted time worrying about things that didn't concern her.

"Nothing fancy," Stacy said. "This is really more of a community get-together than a party. It's just one more chance to see everyone and wish them a 'Merry Christmas' and have Santa Claus come to see the kids."

"Do you think Andrea will come?"

"I don't know. This is my first Christmas here, remember?"

"Well, I think I'll wear my new red dress just in case. You know, I don't think she was at all happy with me last night. All I did was flirt with Drew a little, and he didn't seem to mind at all."

"Why are you intentionally trying to make her dislike you?" Stacy asked.

"I'm not," Joni insisted. "Disliking her has nothing to do with it. We're just having a little friendly competition. The rest of you girls are so nice to each other, Andrea needs someone to keep her on her toes."

Stacy made a face. "If you want to do that, just keep flirting with Lane."

"Really? You mean she's after him, too? This may turn out to be fun after all."

It was a cold, starless night, and a drizzling rain pelted everyone as they entered the old school building that now served as the community center. Every family in Summerdale was represented in the noisy, holiday crowd, but Stacy didn't have any trouble locating Lane. He was standing near the front door talking to Andrea.

Stacy turned away. "Look, there's Tricia and Chuck," she told Joni. "Let's go join them."

"You go ahead," Joni said, already starting toward Lane and Andrea. "I'll catch up later."

Stacy hesitated. There was no telling what Joni might do or say, but whatever it was, she probably wouldn't be able to stop her anyway. She decided to join her friends around the Christmas tree and leave Joni to do what she liked.

"Hi," Tricia said, making room for Stacy in the circle. "Where's Joni?"

"Over there."

Tricia glanced toward the door and raised her eyebrows. "I'll bet that's an interesting conversation. I'd love to know what those three are talking about."

"I wouldn't," Stacy said dryly and changed the subject. "The tree looks great. Where did they find such a large one?"

"It's really two trees," Chuck said. "Lane and I grafted them together this afternoon. If you know where to look, you can see the tape."

"So much for that poem by Joyce Kilmer," Tricia said. "You know, the one that says only God can make a tree."

"He still made it," Chuck said. "We just assembled it."

No one noticed Andrea walking up until she said, "In case you haven't heard, Drew's mother is remarrying, and they're going to move to Pennsylvania right after Christmas. I thought we could have a little farewell party for Drew at our house tonight. Pass the word along to anyone who'd like to come."

"Come where?" Joni asked. She had just walked up, so Andrea reluctantly repeated her invitation.

"Drew's moving to Pennsylvania? That's great," Joni said. "I'll have to make sure he gets a warm welcome. Where is he? Is he coming tonight?"

"Yes, but he said he'd be late," Andrea said.

"I don't mean to change the subject," Tricia said, "I think the idea of having a going-away party for Drew is great, but I wanted to ask y'all about going caroling Christmas Eve? We've never done it before, but we could get all the kids together, even the young ones, and go from house to house."

"Excuse me," Joni said. "I realize I'm not going to be here, but since I have gone caroling before, maybe I should point out one small problem that you might have."

"What's that?" Andrea asked.

"Considering how far apart the houses are, after you walk from one house to the next, you're going to be too out of breath to sing."

"What if we took someone's truck?" Chuck asked.

"A horse-drawn wagon would be even better, especially if it had bells on it," Stacy said. "It wouldn't be a 'one-horse open sleigh,' but it would be the next best thing."

"That's a great idea," Tricia said. "Do y'all want to do it?"

"Sure! It sounds like fun," everyone chorused.

"The Colbys have a wagon. We could probably get Lane to drive it for us," Chuck said.

"It's too bad Joni's not going to be here, she could ask him for us," Andrea said.

"You know, you're right," Joni agreed, "but Stacy's going to be here. Maybe she could ask him."

"Stacy, you're going to be here for Christmas! You mean it? Why didn't you tell me?" Tricia asked without pausing to take a breath.

"You haven't given me a chance. I didn't change my plans until this morning," Stacy said. "I'm staying at Aunt Sara's until Christmas morning, and then I'll go visit Mom and Dad for the week between Christmas and New Year's."

"That's fantastic," Tricia said. "And you do want to go caroling with us, don't you?"

"Of course, I'd love to! Do you still want me to ask Lane about taking us?"

"That's all right. Now that he's alone, I'll ask him myself," Andrea said, flouncing away.

Joni's eyes sparkled mischievously. "You know, it's getting a little chilly in here. Maybe someone should light a fire in that fireplace."

"And have Santa singe his breeches? Shame on you, girl," Chuck said teasingly.

"Who's going to be Santa Claus this year?" someone asked.

"I hope it's not Uncle Jim. Angie would recognize him in a minute," Stacy said.

"It can't be my dad, either," Tricia said. "My little sister is already suspicious."

Just then, Drew hurried up to them. Someone started to ask him about moving to Pennsylvania, but he waved their question away. "Yeah, it's all true, but we'll talk about it later, okay? Right now, Santa has a surprise for the kids, but he needs your help."

"What do we have to do?" Tricia asked.

Drew lowered his voice so that no one would overhear him. "In a few minutes, Mrs. Hogue is going to start leading everyone in singing Christmas carols.

When I give you a signal, pretend that you hear Santa Claus on the roof. Get all the kids to come outside with you."

"But it's raining out there," Stacy protested.

"That makes it even better. We don't want the kids out there very long. Chuck, get your brother, Walter, and help Lane make sure all the kids get outside."

Drew waited for Chuck and Walter to station themselves throughout the crowd and then slipped out of the door. A few minutes after the singing had begun, he came back and waved at Tricia.

"Listen," Tricia cried, her voice carrying through the crowd, "I heard something."

"What? Tiny little hooves?" Hal Colby answered her from the other side of the room.

"Yes! I really think it was," Tricia called back. "Come on, I'm not kidding."

"Let's go see if it's Santa Claus," someone else shouted, and suddenly everyone was hurrying outside.

The clouds had blocked out the stars, but through the tree limbs that draped over part of the old roof, they could see a brightly lit sleigh. While they watched, a figure, dressed in red and carrying a sack over his shoulder, scurried across the roof and disappeared down the chimney.

No one had to hurry the children back inside. They beat most of the adults and caught Santa just as he was dusting the soot off his clothes.

"Ho, ho, ho! Merry Christmas!" he called to them as they gathered around him.

"I take back everything I've ever said against Santa Claus," Joni said. "The first thing I'm going to do when I get home is write out a Christmas list and send it to him."

"This is going to make Angie's Christmas," Stacy said. "She won't believe anything Hal or Chris say against Santa now."

"My head tells me that's really Drew's uncle. I know it because he borrowed Dad's Santa suit. I just can't figure out how he got down that chimney," Andrea said.

"Oh, so that was why Drew was helping," Tricia said.

Drew pushed his way to the center of the group. "Andrea, have you seen Yvette?"

Andrea looked toward the younger crowd. "She was over there with Hal Colby..."

"That was earlier," Drew said. He checked to make sure that there were no little children around before he continued, "Yvette was the Santa up on the roof. We climbed up there this afternoon, and she was the only one small enough to fit inside the chimney."

"I was wondering how your uncle managed that," Tricia said.

"We figured the roof would be far enough away that the kids wouldn't notice the discrepancy in size. There's a small ledge just inside the chimney that Yvette could rest on until we got the kids back inside. She was supposed to climb out and go down the ladder we left behind the building. She was going to sneak into the bathroom and change back into her normal clothes and then join us. She should be back in here by now."

"I'll go check the bathroom. Maybe she's having trouble changing," Tricia said.

Lane had seen Drew looking around the room and sensed something was wrong. He had walked up in time to hear most of the explanation. "We'd better go check the roof," he said.

"I'm almost afraid to find out what she's done now," Andrea said.

"Stacy, maybe you'd better come with us," Lane suggested. "The rest of you make sure none of the little kids come out until we let you know if it's all right."

It was raining harder now, so they paused long enough to grab their coats before following Drew outside. They ran around the building and Lane saw the ladder lying on the ground.

"Yvette," Andrea and Drew called, their voices muffled by the wind and rain. "Where are you? Are you hurt?"

Finally they heard her answer. "I'm up here. In the tree!"

"How did you get over there?" Drew asked.

"I jumped. The ladder fell, and I thought I could get down from the roof by climbing down this tree, but I hurt my foot."

"Can you jump down?" Drew asked. "I'll catch you."

"Get real, Riley," Yvette snorted. "Jumping is how I got into this mess."

Propping the ladder up against the tree, Lane said, "Stacy, go get the flashlight out of my car."

"I'll go up and get her," Drew said. "This wouldn't have happened if I'd stayed out here with her."

When Stacy got back, Drew had started back down with Yvette across his shoulders.

Taking the flashlight from Stacy, Lane said, "Hold the ladder steady, and I'll go see if I can help Drew."

"I'm going to kill my sister," Andrea vowed. "That's what I'm going to do. I'm going to kill her."

When they finally got Yvette on the ground, she was soaking wet and her teeth were chattering.

"Why didn't you call somebody?" Stacy asked.

"I-I d-didn't want the k-kids to hear me."

"So you decided to stay out here and catch pneumonia instead!" Andrea said.

"Look, I'm freezing to death. Do you think you could fuss at me later?" Yvette asked.

"She should go home and get into a hot bath," Lane advised.

"I'll take her," Drew said.

"I'd better go with you," Andrea said quickly.

The rain was coming down harder now, so Lane picked up Yvette while Drew ran ahead to start his car. Following them, Andrea said, "Stacy, will you tell my parents what happened, and remind everyone about coming on over to the house for the uh..." She paused and after a significant glance at Drew, added, "You know."

"I'll take care of it," Stacy promised before Lane grabbed her hand.

"Come on," he ordered. "You're getting wet."

"I'm already wet," she protested as he pulled her along behind him.

They stopped in the alcove to take off their wet coats, and Stacy asked, "If you were so worried about me getting wet, why did you tell me to come out here in the first place?"

She turned away to hang up her coat, and Lane's reply was partly muffled. "I didn't know what we were going to find, and if it turned out to be an emergency, I wanted someone I could count on."

His answer filled Stacy with a warm glow, and she stood absolutely still, her hand still caught in her wet curls. Lane was standing so close she could feel the heat from his body, and the look in his eyes sent her pulse racing.

"I'm a mess," she said nervously. "I really need a mirror."

"You look fine," he said huskily. As if of their own accord, his hands settled on her shoulders and then slid to her back, bringing her even closer.

In some distant part of her mind, Stacy heard her name called, and she put up her hands on Lane's chest to stop him. Lane stiffened and stepped away from her just as Joni and Tricia came through the doorway. Without speaking, he grabbed his coat and went back out into the rain.

Tricia glanced from his dark, angry expression to Stacy's stunned one. "I called you," she said. "Is everything all right?"

Stacy let out her breath with a shaky sigh. "It's fine," she said.

"What about Yvette?"

"Oh...uh, she hurt her foot, but I think she'll be all right. Andrea and Drew took her home."

"Are they still planning to have the party for Drew?"

"Andrea said to remind everyone to come," Stacy said, "but I think I'll skip it."

"Oh, you can't," Tricia said. "You have to put in an appearance."

"I'd really like to go," Joni said. "I want to make sure Drew gets my home address and telephone number. Who knows, we might be able to get together after he moves to Pennsylvania.''

''You and Joni can ride over with Chuck and me. We aren't going to stay very long,'' Tricia said.

''Well, okay. Let me check with Aunt Sara and Uncle Jim and make sure it's all right.''

Tricia turned to go back inside. ''Joni and I'll go let everyone else know that the party's still on, and we'll meet you back here.''

Chapter Twelve

Before they left the community center, Stacy and Joni helped Chuck and Tricia clean and put everything back in order. When they finally arrived at the Broussards', the house was alive with lights and music.

When Stacy saw Yvette sitting beside the fireplace with her injured ankle wrapped in an elastic bandage and supported by a footstool, she went over to see her.

"How's your foot?" she asked.

Yvette wiggled her toes and rotated her ankle slowly. "I think I just twisted it. Mom said that if it looks worse tomorrow, she'd take me in for X rays. I don't think she's too thrilled about having two of us on crutches at Christmas."

"That's right," Stacy said. "I heard that Gary was getting out of the hospital for Christmas. How's he doing?"

"The doctor said his foot would be as good as new by spring. If something like that was going to happen, I guess we were lucky it happened when it did. Dad's not too busy, and now that Drew's leaving . . ."

Drew grabbed Yvette from behind. "Did I hear you say it was *lucky* that I was leaving?" he asked.

"Well, at least I won't get banged up trying to carry out any more of your harebrained ideas," she said.

"*My* harebrained ideas? You planned that stunt on top of the roof!" Drew said accusingly. "The only reason I helped you was because you threatened to do it by yourself if I didn't."

"I don't know whose idea it was, and I'm really sorry that you got hurt, but I have to tell you—the kids loved it," Stacy told them. "Angie's convinced that Santa can come down a chimney, and I even saw Chris checking it out."

"Well, it really was my idea," Yvette said smugly and then ducked as Drew feigned a blow at her head.

"If Santa didn't really come down the chimney, how did he get in?" Stacy asked.

"When the kids ran outside, Uncle Mike just climbed in through the window and ran over to the fireplace," Drew said.

"How did he get back out? I didn't see him leave."

"That's what we were counting on," Drew said. "While the kids were busy with their presents and everyone was watching them, the men crowded around Santa until they blocked him from view. When they were sure he was hidden, he climbed back out the window."

"I admit—that part was Drew's idea," Yvette said.

"We're going to miss you around here," Stacy told him. "It's not going to be the same."

"If I had my way, I'd stay," Drew said, "but at least Mom's happy. And who knows? Maybe I'll get to like Pennsylvania as much as you like it here."

"I know Joni will be more than happy to help you. She said she wanted to give you her home address and telephone number before she left."

"I'll make a point to see her," Drew said, grinning slyly. "As soon as she's through talking to Lane."

Stacy refused to look in the direction Drew indicated. She had no idea that Lane was going to be here. When he left the community center, she had assumed he was going home. And if he'd come over here to see Andrea, why was he with Joni?

As if Stacy's thoughts had conjured her up, Andrea suddenly appeared at Yvette's side. "Stacy, could you help me in the kitchen for a minute?"

"Sure," Stacy said, giving up her place at Drew's side to someone else.

In the kitchen Mrs. Broussard was busy putting the finishing touches on a cake for Drew, so Andrea led Stacy to the other side of the room. She began putting more cookies on some empty trays, and Stacy, not knowing what else to do, followed her lead.

Andrea shook her head. "That's okay. I didn't really need any help. I just wanted a chance to thank you privately."

"For helping with Yvette? I didn't do anything except get the flashlight."

"I wasn't talking about that," Andrea said. "Yvette told me that you helped get me a date for the Christmas dance."

Andrea's cheeks were flaming, and Stacy could feel her own growing warm. "Oh, that," she said. "It wasn't anything."

"Not to you maybe, but can you imagine what people would have said if they knew the Key Club's Sweetheart didn't have a date for the dance?"

"Andrea, I never thought you couldn't get a date. As soon as I found out that you and Joni both thought you had a date with Lane, I knew there had to be some kind of misunderstanding."

"I've already talked to Lane, and we've cleared everything up," Andrea said. "He told me to save him a dance, and I thought he was asking me to be his date for the dance. I guess I just heard what I wanted to."

"Don't worry about it." Stacy made a mental note to swear Tricia to secrecy. "No one else even knows it happened."

"That's another thing I want to thank you for," Andrea said. "Since this is the time for 'Peace on earth and good will toward men,' I thought it would be a good time to let you know I appreciate it. After the beginning of the new year, it's going to be back to business as usual."

Stacy met Andrea's smile with one of her own. "Thanks for the warning," she said.

Mrs. Broussard finished with Drew's cake, and Andrea carried it into the family room and led everyone in a chorus of "For He's a Jolly Good Fellow."

Embarrassed, Drew gave a short speech and then made a great show of helping cut and pass out pieces of the cake.

Stacy drifted around the room, talking to Regina Dawson and Walter Hastings, Chuck's brother, and some of her other friends. She answered questions about Joni and repeated her plans to stay in Summerdale until Christmas Day.

She made a complete circle around the room before she realized she hadn't seen Chuck or Tricia. They weren't in the family room or the kitchen. She turned to go into the living room, and not watching where she was going, she walked right into Lane.

"I'm sorry," she mumbled, not quite able to look him in the eyes. "I was looking for Tricia and Chuck."

"They left a few minutes ago," he said.

"They couldn't," she said. "Joni and I are supposed to ride home with them."

"Joni just left with Drew."

"She... what?"

"Come on, I'll take you home," he said.

"No, that's all right. I'll get a ride with..."

Lane ignored her objections and took her elbow. "Where's your coat?" he asked.

"I left it by the front door," Stacy said, "but really, you don't have to do this."

Lane steered her through the crowd toward the front door, pausing just long enough to grab her jacket from the pile on the chair beside the door.

The rain had turned to sleet, leaving icy patches on the highway and making it necessary for Lane to concentrate on his driving. Stacy didn't mind. While he concentrated on the highway, she could concentrate on him, and from the headlights of a passing car, she could see the muscle in his cheek twitch as he clenched and unclenched his jaw.

She didn't know why he had insisted on taking her home, but she wasn't surprised by the tautness of his voice when he finally spoke. "Joni told me you were glad that we broke up."

Stacy caught her breath. "She told you that?"

"What's the matter? Was it supposed to be a secret?"

"No, but I didn't mean it like that."

With a sharp turn of the steering wheel, Lane swung into the driveway. "How many ways can you mean something like that?" he asked, his voice heavy with sarcasm as he shifted the car into park and switched off the engine.

"All I meant was that it gave me some time to think—to make some of my own decisions."

"Such as?"

"Why do you care? I thought—"

Lane cut her off. "Stacy, tell me."

"All right," Stacy said. "I was tired of you and Mom telling me what I wanted. Mom thought you were the only reason I was staying in Summerdale, and you accused me of wanting to move back to Philadelphia. I decided it was time I figured out what I wanted for myself."

The car was quiet except for the sound of Lane's indrawn breath. "What did you decide?"

"I've really been happy here, but I'm a little too old to think that I can live with Aunt Sara for the rest of my life. Then it came to me—I don't have to. I have my own house right here in Summerdale."

Stacy wanted to make sure that he understood that it was her decision and that it didn't involve him. "I'm going to college first. Everyone needs to be able to support herself somehow, but then I'm coming back to live in Summerdale. It's my home."

Without a word, Lane reached across her and opened the glove compartment. He took out an envelope and dropped it on her lap.

"What's this?" she asked.

"My airline ticket. I was going to follow you to Philadelphia and drag you back here if I had to."

Stacy stared at the tickets and then lifted her eyes to his face. "But you told Mom you didn't care if I left."

"You know me better than to believe something like that! What I told your mother was that I wouldn't stand in your way if you wanted to leave—and even that was a lie. I didn't know it at the time, but I could never let you go."

"I never wanted to," she said softly.

Before Stacy finished speaking, she was in his arms, and he was kissing her.

When he finally released her, Stacy buried her head in the hollow of his shoulder, and Lane nuzzled her hair. "This has been the worst month of my life. I don't even know how I'm going to stand it when you go away to college," he said.

"It won't be so bad," she murmured.

His arms tightened around her. "Then you obviously don't know how I feel."

"Yes, I do, but I've made some other decisions, too. I'll be going to college somewhere locally. I should be able to come home a couple of times a semester."

"And you won't mind if I come to see you?"

"I'll mind if you don't," she said. Remembering the tickets, she asked, "What about Philadelphia? Will you still come? I want you to meet my father, and I'd like to show you around."

"I'll follow you anywhere," he said huskily.

He kissed her again, and Stacy said, "It's getting late. I really should go inside."

Lane kept his arm around her all the way to the door. "I just got you back. I hate to let you go again," he said. "I won't see you again until after Christmas."

Suddenly Stacy realized that Lane didn't know she had changed her plans. She opened her mouth to tell him but caught herself. He didn't need to know everything at once. "It won't be long," she whispered instead.

"One day is too long," he muttered. "I'll trade shifts with Jim. He can milk tomorrow morning, and I'll come by and take you to the airport."

"No," Stacy said quickly. "Don't do that. I don't want to say goodbye to you in a crowded airport. Besides, Uncle Jim promised Angie and Chris that they could come with us, and he'd take them to do their Christmas shopping afterward. I'd hate to disappoint them."

"What about me?"

Stacy smiled. "I'll talk to Santa and see if he'll bring you something special for Christmas."

"There's only one thing I want, and I don't think even Santa Claus can get it for me," he said before he kissed her again. "I love you, Stacy. I really do."

They held each other for a minute, and then Lane opened his arms and let her go inside the house.

Joni was waiting up for her, and she smiled when she saw the stars in her friend's eyes. "I take it you and Lane made up," she said.

"How did you know?" Stacy asked.

"Well, I figured he had something in mind when he ran us off from the party."

"What do you mean? Who did he run off?"

"Well, me for one. And Chuck and Tricia. He was making pretty sure that you'd have to go home with him."

"I wonder why," Stacy said.

Joni gave an elaborate shrug. "I don't have the faintest idea. One minute I'm talking to him, telling him how glad you were that you and he had broken up..."

"You mean you told him that on purpose?"

"Now, don't get upset. I talked it over with Tricia, and she and I agreed that we had to do something to get you two talking again. We figured that once you did—well, things would just take care of themselves. And you have to admit, we were right, weren't we?"

"Were you ever!" Stacy said. "I don't know how to thank you."

"Just think of it as a Christmas present," Joni said. "I suppose Lane's glad that you're staying a few more days."

Stacy smiled. "He doesn't know it yet, but he will."

Since Hal had already agreed to help Lane at the barn while everyone else took Joni to the airport, Stacy set her alarm so that she could get up in time to catch him before he left the next morning.

"How would you like to switch places with me today?" she asked him when he came into the kitchen.

"You mean, you'll milk for me, and I'll..."

"Go make sure that Joni gets on her plane to Philadelphia all right," Stacy said.

"I take it you and Lane made up?"

Stacy nodded happily. "Last night."

"I'm glad about that," he said, and then grinned. "But I don't know about this other. You're asking an awful lot. If I ride all the way to Sheffield with Joni, I might even have to hug her when I say goodbye."

"And don't forget to get my ticket changed," Stacy added.

"Well, in that case, I guess I can do it, but what about you? Don't you want to tell Joni goodbye?"

"I told her last night," Stacy said. "She knows what I'm doing."

Hal shook his head. "If love makes you want to spend your mornings in a cold, wet dairy barn, I hope I never fall in love."

Stacy smiled back at him as she pulled on her coat. "You'll change your mind one of these days."

When she got to the barn, Lane was already there. He didn't look up, but at the sound of footsteps, he barked, "You're late! Hurry up and wipe down the feed trough."

"Yes, sir," she snapped. "I'll get right to it."

He whirled around, his blue eyes brilliant against his tanned face. "What . . . what are you doing here?"

"Getting ready to feed the cows. You just told me . . ."

"I know what I said, but I wasn't talking to you," Lane said, illogically. He walked purposefully toward her.

Stacy started to back up. "Who else is there?" she asked. "Of course, if you'd rather have someone else help you, I can go back home and see if Hal . . ."

"That's not what I want and you know it," he said, capturing her in a fierce hug. He lifted her completely off the floor and buried his face in her hair. "I thought your plane left this morning," he said huskily.

"No, just Joni's. I changed my reservations so I won't have to leave until Christmas Day."

He kissed the top of her head, her temple and her cheek, working his way toward her lips. "I guess there really is a Santa Claus,'' he murmured. ''I just got what I wanted for Christmas.''

Stacy pulled back as far as Lane's arms would allow. ''The cows,'' she reminded him. ''Hadn't we better get started milking? You said we were already late.''

''Then a few more minutes won't make any difference,'' he said, drawing her close to him again.

Stacy smiled, letting her love shine through her eyes. ''I guess not,'' she said, raising her lips to meet his.

* * * * *